Renovating Hearts

by

Kira Anderson

Renovating Hearts

Cover Art by *Kim Mendoza*

The Wild Rose Press, Inc.
PO Box 708
Adams Basin, NY 14410-0708
Visit us at www.thewildrosepress.com

Publishing History
First Edition, 2021
Trade Paperback ISBN 978-1-5092-3921-4
Digital ISBN 978-1-5092-3922-1

Published in the United States of America

Sydney removed and unfolded the piece of notebook paper. As was customary, the receptionist or interns opened her fan mail first and read each letter, checking for legitimacy. Those envelopes were always put on her desk, so how had Becca gotten this one or worse yet, Marv Wilson, the executive producer? She smiled at the childish scrawl and the crude stick figure holding a power drill.

Dear Miss Sydney Ryan,

We watch your show every week. My daddy says you're very talented and can make any place shine brand new. I need your help. Our restaurant is not doing so well, and I can hear my daddy talking about it with my uncle when he thinks I'm not listening. It has been in our family since way before I was born. Even before my daddy was born. Please come and fix our café. I would ask Santa, but I don't think he'd do as good of a job and he's busy right now with Christmas and everything. I want to see my daddy smile again. I would be forever grateful.

Love,

Mary-Katerina Quinn

Sydney slapped the letter onto a manila folder on Becca's desk. She frowned and shook her head. "Oh, no you don't. I'm done filming for this year. I've earned this time off. I'm spending Christmas in the Caymans, remember? I have my plane tickets and my hotel reservation. I'm ready for sandy beaches, piña coladas, and rest and relaxation. I've earned it."

Praise for Kira Anderson

RENOVATING HEARTS is a feel-good story showcasing the importance of letting people in and allowing love to find you. Kira creates images of idyllic winter scenery and warm, compassionate characters that will draw in readers. This is a "can't miss" holiday book!

~Nicki K.

~*~

RENOVATING HEARTS made me feel warm and cozy like a cup of hot chocolate on a cold day. I could picture the snow and small-town scenery. The characters came alive, and I became immersed in their stories and couldn't wait for the happy ending. RENOVATING HEARTS was an entertaining and heartwarming story. I look forward to more from this author!

~Lauren D.

~*~

What a delightful story! I enjoyed the interaction and insight of the lead characters with all characters of the story. Well written…a fun tale of both family and romantic love!

~Sandy S.

~*~

RENOVATING HEARTS is a well-written, fun journey. The male characters and strong women had depth and deep emotion. I smiled and by Chapter Seven I was in tears. Kira is a true word crafter and I applaud this book.

~Nancy D.

Dedication

For Shane and Emily

Chapter One

"Sydney Ryan, my office," Becca Montgomery barked as she swept past.

When Sydney looked up from her cluttered desk wedged in the cramped office between the break room and the broom closet, she caught a glimpse of the brunette in the red dress. At least Sydney had her own space where she could shut out the world for five minutes when she worked in her Los Angeles office. Most of the time she spent on location for her show, *Ryan to the Rescue,* where she turned failing restaurants into chic, must-go destinations. She eyed the pile of fan letters overflowing her inbox. They'd have to wait, but she'd get to them because she replied to each one. During that time, she'd enjoy six weeks in the office before her next scheduled filming in Santa Fe, New Mexico.

"Be right there." Sydney's words fell on deaf ears. Her producer disappeared. After another gaze at the screen saver of a pristine white, sandy beach, turquoise water, and empty chaise lounge chairs under a red umbrella, she locked her computer. Four weeks and counting. Christmas in the Caymans couldn't come soon enough.

"Sit." A minute later, Becca motioned toward the high-back, black leather chair before she searched through the stack of papers on her desk.

Sydney moved the pile of magazines to the floor and plopped down. While her office was neat, Becca's window let in the sunlight. Sydney gazed past the palm trees lining Wilshire Boulevard to the four-story, concrete-and-glass office building across the way. Holding a cup of coffee, crazy tie guy stood at the window of his oversized office and waved. She wiggled her fingers and shifted in her seat the longer Becca rummaged around. Despite the mess, her producer prided herself on organization. Sydney suspected she would not like whatever she found. Becca also wasn't always so tired, scatterbrained, or short tempered. She'd also added a few pounds. "What's up?"

"I just had them in Wilson's office." Becca flipped through the pages in her leather day planner. "Here they are. Read this and we'll talk." She pulled out two envelopes and handed her the top one.

Sydney removed and unfolded the piece of notebook paper. As was customary, the receptionist or interns opened her fan mail first and read each letter, checking for legitimacy. Those envelopes were always put on her desk, so how had Becca gotten this one or worse yet, Marv Wilson, the executive producer? She smiled at the childish scrawl and the crude stick figure holding a power drill.

Dear Miss Sydney Ryan,

We watch your show every week. My daddy says you're very talented and can make any place shine brand new. I need your help. Our restaurant is not doing so well, and I can hear my daddy talking about it with my uncle when he thinks I'm not listening. It has been in our family since way before I was born. Even before my daddy was born. Please come and fix our café. I would ask Santa, but I don't think he'd do as good of a job and he's busy right now with Christmas and everything. I want to see my daddy smile again. I would be forever grateful.

Love,

Mary-Katerina Quinn

Sydney slapped the letter onto a manila folder on Becca's desk. She frowned and shook her head. "Oh, no you don't. I'm done filming for this year. I've earned this time off. I'm spending Christmas in the Caymans, remember? I have my plane tickets and my hotel reservation. I'm ready for sandy beaches, piña coladas, and rest and relaxation. I've earned it."

Becca scrunched her eyebrows together, pursed her lips, and played with a pen.

The clicking noise grated on Sydney's nerves.

"I know what you planned. The Caymans this year. Where were you last year? New Zealand?"

"No. Maui. New Zealand was the year before."

Tapping pointer fingers against her lips, Becca stared. "You should stick around Los Angeles for Christmas. You might enjoy it."

She crossed her arms, ignoring the compassion in Becca's eyes. "We have this discussion every year. I'm working off all the items on my bucket list while I'm young enough to enjoy them."

"You're avoiding the holidays. We both know it."

Becca threw her pen back in the soup can decorated with colorful tissue paper and sequins her oldest son, Carson, made.

The irritation in Becca's voice surprised Sydney. Usually mild-mannered and accommodating, Becca's sudden action unleashed a few butterflies in her stomach.

"You can always join my family. We'd love to have you." Becca spoke in a quiet voice.

The old Becca returned, soothing Sydney's unease. Sydney roved her gaze over the recent portrait of Becca, her husband, Vincent, her five-year-old son Carson, and three-year-old daughter, Tabitha, dressed in matching sweaters. Her producer was lucky. Her husband worked from home, and they had a live-in nanny to take care of everything. When Tabitha was born, Becca negotiated to stay in L.A. and send her assistant to help with the on-site production. Not every kid was so fortunate. "I appreciate the gesture, but I have my reasons."

"Okay. Suit yourself. Never say I didn't invite you. As for this plea?" Becca picked up the letter and stared at it, lines creasing her forehead. "I tried to get Wilson to change his mind. Believe me, I'm not happy either, but after he saw this letter, he doesn't like the line-up."

Sydney stood and paced the office confines. Six steps on the beige carpeting to get from the bookcase filled with tapes and awards to the Ficus tree and the wall covered with posters of Becca's productions. "What does he want from me?"

"You're to go to Colorado, track down this Mary-Katerina Quinn, get permission from the father to do the makeover, so we can air the episode December twenty-third."

"That's impossible." Sydney ran a hand through her hair, finding it hard to breathe in the stale air-conditioned air. "Production takes weeks, and I've already scouted the location and designed the improvements long before I arrive for the shooting."

4

Becca grabbed the other envelope. "You've done it before. Remember the Mexican place in Houston? That production took three weeks, so nothing is impossible. I'm counting on you. You've got less than four weeks. Your plane ticket to Denver, directions to Silver Ridge, and the hotel and rental car information are inside. Because of Thanksgiving, I couldn't get you out any earlier than Saturday."

"What if I refuse?" Sydney had never done that before. She and Becca discussed each project and agreed on which ones would work and problems that might arise during production. This time, based on a child's letter, her producer and executive producer decided without her input.

"Don't disappoint us, Sydney. Who can resist a heartfelt plea from a young girl at Christmas to rescue her father's restaurant with the backdrop of the Rocky Mountains, snow, and a quaint, old-fashioned town at Christmas? The crew flies out next Saturday, giving you a week to find this child, get permission, and finalize your concept. The show airs before the holidays, so unless you change your mind and join my family for Christmas, you can still make your beach vacation."

****

"Here you go. I love snow, don't you?"

Excitement and awe hovered in the young girl's voice as she set down the cup of coffee. Her question interrupted Sydney's thoughts as she sat at the table and gazed at the falling snow outside Joe's Café in Silver Ridge, Colorado. Tired from her early morning flight and too soon to check into the hotel, Sydney stopped in for a cup of coffee. "Thank you. Snow has its purpose, I suppose." She scanned the light blanket of white dusting the ground and trees and her rental car, the only vehicle in the parking lot. A wet cold she hadn't felt before permeated her light winter jacket, and she shuddered as she ripped open a package of sugar and dumped the contents into her coffee. Then she poured in a dollop of cream.

The girl hovered by her table.

Sydney should be in L.A., answering fan mail and dreaming about her beach vacation, not freezing in some Podunk town in the middle of Colorado. Her producer and executive producer had other ideas, and now she sat here, freezing like the white dots floating past the window.

"Did you know all snowflakes are different?"

The girl wanted to talk, which suited Sydney. The chatter gave her something else to think about. "I'd heard that a long time ago. Amazing, don't you think? Of all the millions of snowflakes, none are identical." Sydney turned and smiled at the girl, with dark brown hair pulled back in a sloppy ponytail and brown, expressive eyes, and guessed her to be eight. The coffee cup's warmth against her chilled hands matched the heat from the burning logs in the rustic river stone fireplace behind her.

The quaint café intrigued her. A smart, crisp white tablecloth with a single flower in a bud vase would spruce up the place and hide the well-used wood table with scar marks etched into the surface. New chairs and a fresh coat of paint along with historic pictures of the small town would welcome and encourage customers to linger in the old train depot.

After another quick glance around the empty, faded

interior, she wondered how it stayed in business. Not her concern. She had to find Mary-Katerina Quinn, get her father to agree to the show, and film it so she could relax in the Caymans over the holidays.

"God told all his angels to make each snowflake unique, just like he makes all his creatures different. One of a kind."

Before she took another sip of coffee, Sydney looked at the girl and smiled. "That's very insightful. Who told you that?" A proud expression flickered across the little girl's face.

"My mom."

"Your mom is a very smart woman. Is she here?" Aside from the girl standing next to the table, Sydney hadn't seen an employee in the café. Where were the adults?

"She's in Heaven. Daddy says she helps the other angels make the snow because she knows I like to make snow angels and build snowmen. When I do, I think of her."

"I'm sorry to hear that." Her throat tightened, and unshed tears filled her eyes. No child should grow up motherless. Sydney knew firsthand life wasn't fair. She glanced outside again, the snowflakes multiplying faster and gaining ground on the barren earth. "If the snow keeps up, you can do that tomorrow." Swallowing her sorrow, she kept her voice light, her heart aching for the girl.

"I've been praying for snow. My mom must be listening."

Sydney reached for her hand and squeezed. "She is. And when you have her in your heart, she'll always be there for you." Another smile rose to Sydney's lips.

"Sometimes it helps to have a reminder, even if other people are unhappy like those who have to drive in this stuff."

Snow added a complication. Sydney grew up in L.A. and didn't have much driving experience in the white stuff, but her bosses insisted. Surviving the next few weeks stuck in Silver Ridge would be a challenge, but she'd faced one or two or twenty in her life.

No one went against Wilson if he or she wanted to tape another season. *Ryan to the Rescue* was her baby, and her pride and joy. New contract negotiations for *Ryan to the Rescue* started soon, and Becca hinted at a possible five-year contract this time with a substantial increase in money per episode. Her ratings were great, and Sydney could save more money in order to open her own restaurant in the future.

So, although she didn't appreciate having no input into the decision, why question the executive producer? In a town this size, she should easily find Mary-Katerina Quinn, meet her father, and convince him to let her do the show.

The girl pulled out the next chair, sat, and held out a hand. "Hi. Daddy says I'm rude if I don't introduce myself to new customers. I'm Molly Ransom from Silver Ridge, Colorado. Pleased to meet you. We hope you like our establishment and come back often."

Her words confirmed what Sydney had already guessed, and she grinned at the precociousness of Molly's words that seemed way beyond her years. She shook her hand. "I'm Sydney Ryan from Los Angeles. You may call me Ms. Sydney. Pleased to meet you, too, and I'll come here as often as I can."

"Sydney Ryan?" Molly squeaked and her eyes

widened. Her mouth formed a perfect O.

The girl's priceless reaction warmed her heart.

"Sydney Ryan? From *Ryan to the Rescue*? I thought you looked familiar. But you look so different. I mean—I wasn't sure. You always have your hair in braids. I mean why would—it worked! UNCLE RAY, THE LETTER WORKED!" Molly jumped from her seat, knocking over her wooden chair. She lifted her arms and twirled across the floor. Then she ran back, wrapped her arms around Sydney's neck, and squeezed. "I knew you would come."

"So, you're Mary-Katerina Quinn?" Unwrapping the girl's arms from her neck, Sydney laughed. With her first order of business complete, she'd already thought of ideas to update the interior. If the rest fell in line, in four weeks she'd be on the beach drinking a piña colada and crossing another destination off her bucket list.

"Yes!" Molly puffed out her chest. "They named me after both my grandmothers and Quinn was for me. But it's too hard to say, so they call me Molly."

"Those names are a mouthful. Molly suits you better."

Shaking, Molly picked up her chair, sat, and rested her chin on her cupped hands.

Freckles graced her nose and cheeks, and long eyelashes rimmed her wide, expressive eyes.

"My dad and I watch your show every week. All my friends, too." She chatted on. "Even my Uncle Ray watches it. He's the one who helped me with the letter."

"A refill, Ms. Ryan?" An elderly man with a full head of white hair materialized with a pot of coffee.

"Yes, please." She held out her cup.

A slow grin crossed his wrinkled features.

"I just made sure she had the studio address and a stamp. Ray Donaldson." He shifted the pot into his left hand. "Pleased to meet you."

"Likewise. Please, call me Sydney." She took his proffered hand. The faint conspiratorial look that passed between the man and Molly made Sydney wonder if the idea hadn't been his. It didn't matter. Molly wrote the letter, and once Wilson made a decision, an earthquake couldn't derail him from making it happen.

With her eye on a new contract, Sydney would, too. She found the child; she found the restaurant, and it needed a lot of changes. She and her designer, Emily, had their work cut out for them. She blew wispy bangs from her eyes. Now, she needed permission from the father which shouldn't be an issue since he watched the show and was familiar with the process. She could almost taste the coconut concoction and feel the sun's heat against her skin as she lazed around on the beach.

Molly pushed a piece of hair that escaped her ponytail behind her ear and beamed. "I can't believe it. You read my letter, and now you're here. Daddy will be so surprised."

Her beach scene morphed into the dismal white floating past the window. Her father didn't know about the letter?

****

Jack Ransom turned the knob and shouldered the back door to Joe's Cafe, his hands filled with a stack of mail from the post office box. Nothing but invoices and bills. He brushed the snow from the envelopes and the sleeve of his jacket, the warm interior a nice contrast to the falling temperatures outside.

One car in the parking lot meant paying customers. Tourists, judging by the out-of-state plate and the rental company barcode on the window. He'd take what money he could get. Business had been slow for the past year, and if he wanted to keep the café open, he needed to generate more business.

To his right, Uncle Ray wiped down the prep counter, his white hair a striking contrast to the red brick wall behind him. Through the small window in the kitchen door to the main part of the restaurant, he was surprised to see a tall blonde braiding his daughter's hair. He'd tried arranging Molly's unruly curls into a passable ponytail this morning, but the strands refused to cooperate. When he caught the woman's profile, he swallowed and blinked.

Impossible. Everyone in Silver Ridge would notice the minute a celebrity set foot inside town. She was a look-alike. After dropping the mail on the side counter, he motioned Uncle Ray closer. Sometimes, his late father's best friend forgot to turn on his hearing aid. "Thanks for covering for me this afternoon. The weather's bad out there. Go home. I'll close up."

"Works for me." Uncle Ray untied his apron and folded it into a tiny white square. Then he wrapped the strings around the middle and wedged the apron under the counter. "I doubt we'll get any more customers today, anyway."

"Did we have any others?"

"Two others besides the woman who ordered a cup of coffee. She's still here, fixing Molly's hair." He lowered his gruff voice yet kept his gaze toward the restaurant interior. "I'm worried, Jack. You need to drum up business. You need help."

11

An expression crossed Uncle Ray's deep-lined features but disappeared before Jack deciphered it. He pulled off his brown, winter carpenter's hat and scraped a hand through his hair. The café had struggled for the past few years. His wife's death sucked out the life. His marginal day consisted of regular customers and a few tourists like the blonde. He patted Uncle Ray's back. "I have a hard time paying my bills as it is. I can't afford an overpriced consultant to tell me everything I'm doing wrong. I'll figure it out." Jack slumped his shoulders. He needed a miracle and soon.

Uncle Ray shrugged into his coat. "Sure you will. Don't wait too long. The answer might be closer than you think."

"Good night, Uncle Ray. Drive safe."

"You, too. Count the drawer and lock up. Take Molly home before the roads get too bad."

Jack nodded. His bungalow was only six blocks away, but the snow would make driving treacherous. Since business was slow, counting the cash and locking it in the safe would be easy.

Uncle Ray cracked the door. "Goodbye, Molly. See you tomorrow."

"Bye, Uncle Ray."

His uncle disappeared into a sea of white before Jack questioned why he didn't thank his last customer for coming in as was customary for his staff. His uncle's strange actions over the past few weeks concerned Jack. Did Uncle Ray need to visit his doctor?

He stared out the tiny window again, searching for a spouse or boyfriend. No one. He didn't see many single tourists these days. If they stopped in town, they didn't come here. Time to get her moving so he could lock up.

Agitated from the conversation with his uncle, Jack struck the swinging door. It banged against the wall and echoed in the almost-empty room. In the dining area, his daughter's laughter mingled with the woman's, the sound foreign to his ears. Molly had little to be happy about lately because Jack wasn't the best of company. His daughter paid the price during the three years Jack became both father and mother to her while working six days a week.

Molly grinned from ear to ear. "Daddy, look who's here. It's Sydney Ryan from *Ryan to the Rescue*. See what she did to my hair?"

She twirled before she wrapped her arms around his waist. An immaculate french braid hung down her back. He swallowed, but not from the memory of his late wife doing the same thing for their daughter. "It looks great, honey." Jack forced the words past stiff lips.

Disentangling herself, she tugged at Jack's hand, pulling him across the room. "Come meet Ms. Sydney. It's *her,* Dad, from *Ryan to the Rescue*."

Quelling the churning in his stomach Jack held out a hand to the woman standing at the corner table. "Welcome, Sydney Ryan. Jack Ransom. I see you've met my daughter." For a moment, he forgot to breathe. The camera didn't showcase her raw beauty. Her deep green eyes were the same color gracing the tree leaves on the mountainsides surrounding Silver Ridge. Jack chose not to get lost in them. He had no time or energy for Sydney or any woman. He needed to focus on the café and keeping it open for another fifty years, for his grandchildren to run as he did for his grandparents who founded it.

"Yes, she's an astounding and thoughtful child. You're a lucky man, Mr. Ransom."

"Thank you." She accepted the handshake.

An unwanted jolt of electricity charged his nerve endings. His late wife's petite stature contrasted Sydney Ryan's who stood only a few inches shorter than his six-foot-one frame. She didn't look as tall on TV. Marin's long, dark hair matched the warm color of her eyes. The woman's tint reminded him of spun gold, and she kept the length cropped just below her shoulders. She always wore it in braids on her show, but the style suited her. Her clothing spoke of Los Angeles fashion, not the tiny community of Silver Ridge where the sidewalks rolled up at eight o'clock on the weeknights and eleven most weekends. "What brings you to our little town?"

"I got the most amazing fan letter."

The woman's smile lit up the darkening room as she shifted her gaze between him and his daughter. Molly flourished under her attention. Even the interior seemed brighter, more inviting. A spiral of dread burst inside his stomach. Molly *had* been up to something. She wasn't good at secrets. Sydney Ryan inside his restaurant was not a coincidence and only meant one thing.

Marin's vision flitted through his mind, but with each passing day, the image faded. Too many other things competed, like keeping the café open. He wished she hadn't died. He needed her sound advice. His daughter meant well, but for her to go behind his back and contact Sydney Ryan was a complication he didn't need.

More days like today and he would close his doors by spring.

Molly tugged on his flannel shirt. "Daddy, I wrote Ms. Sydney a letter and asked her to help you. I can't believe she's here."

"Me, either." His daughter's emotion set him on edge because her happiness would be short-lived. Molly should have told him about her pie-in-the-sky scheme. Jack dug Joe's Café into a hole, so he would fix it. Again, he scraped a hand through his hair. He had enough to worry about. "Why did you do that without my permission?"

"Because I wanted to surprise you. Mrs. Collins said—"

"Mrs. Collins is in on this plot?" He clenched his teeth as his stomach debated on whether to accept or reject his earlier piece of toast.

Molly widened her eyes. "Yes, even Uncle Ray—"

Unable to remain in one spot, Jack paced. "Uncle Ray? He should know better, too." Now he understood the glances between the two, and why his uncle acted strange over the past few weeks. Uncle Ray had no right to contact Sydney Ryan, and her network had no right to send out the reality TV star without consulting him first.

"Daddy, aren't you happy?" Moisture filled Molly's eyes, and her bottom lip wobbled.

His heartbeat increased as sweat gathered on his palms. Heat seared the back of his neck. His uncle's words earlier made sense. Sydney Ryan was not the solution to his problem. His precocious daughter meant well, and he felt honored she cared so much about the family restaurant and about him, but he wasn't. "No, honey, I'm not. I can't believe you contacted her."

Molly wiped the tears from her cheeks. "But, Daddy…"

He shot his gaze back to Sydney who looked so confident, so natural standing inside his place, he blinked to make sure she wasn't a mirage. No such luck. "So, do you always make a personal appearance to thank the sender?"

"No. I usually send a letter, but this is a special case. I wanted to thank Molly in person for bringing this charming place to my attention." Sydney retrieved a white, two-pocket folder from her over-sized bag. "Please review and sign the paperwork so my crew and I can start work next week. We're on a tight schedule."

Jack frowned. He'd rather not talk about this situation in front of Molly, but he had no choice. His daughter would learn a valuable lesson. Sydney Ryan, too. He crossed his arms, refusing the folder. "You should have called. You've come to Silver Ridge on a wild goose chase, Ms. Ryan. I'll never allow you to film an episode here. Sorry, but you've wasted your time."

Chapter Two

"No, Daddy, please." Tears flowed down Molly's cheeks. Molly ran to Sydney and buried her face in her light blue sweater.

Jack watched Sydney cradle Molly and pat her on the back, her soft mew calming his daughter.

"All I wanted to do was help, Ms. Sydney. He works and worries too much. He thinks I can't hear him talking to Uncle Ray, but I can. Even Uncle Ray liked the idea."

"I know you did, sweetheart. Some people don't want help. Your father is one of them."

Sydney's soothing voice filled the tense air. A myriad of emotions flickered across her feminine features. She glanced at the delicate gold watch gracing her slender wrist before she schooled her expression and gazed between him and his daughter.

She smiled. "I don't consider coming here a waste of my time, Mr. Ransom. I wouldn't have had the pleasure of visiting Silver Ridge, seeing your place, and meeting Molly, and that was worth it." Sydney squatted and dried Molly's tears before she tugged on her braid and tapped her on the nose. She stood again and tucked the white folder back in her bag. "I'll be on my way. For now."

Molly stomped a foot. "Daddy, no! Let her stay! She hasn't finished her coffee."

"Don't worry, Molly. I'll get more at the hotel."

"But that's not what we believe in, you said so, Daddy. 'When you're here, you're part of our family.' See? Where are your manners?" Shaking her head, Molly pointed toward the hand-painted sign over the counter before she crossed her arms, jutting out her bottom lip.

He sensed another meltdown. Leave it to his eight-year-old daughter to point out the obvious. This woman made him lose all sense of reason. "My apologies, Ms. Ryan. Would you care for a cup of coffee to go?"

To avoid staring, he gazed out the window. Tension coiled in his gut. Skeleton tree limbs creaked beneath the flurries swirling in the air. A wall of white descended, blocking the mountains beyond the town limits. The weather forecasters were right when they predicted a blizzard. If this snow kept up, they'd have a foot by morning, and business would suffer.

"No thanks, Mr. Ransom, I've had enough."

The warmth in her voice surprised him when he'd given her no reason to be happy. Well, he wasn't too pleased either.

"I should leave before the snow gets too deep and I can't move my car."

Like the lone leaf on the tree outside the window, he struggled to hold on in the raging storm. He fought to remain standing in one place when all he wanted to do was show her the door so he could close and take Molly home. "Right. You wouldn't get far in this blizzard."

A soft chuckle escaped Sydney's lips, and she blushed.

"Especially since I don't have a lot of experience.

18

If driving in this stuff is like ice skating, I wouldn't be returning much of the rental car."

Her amusement surprised him. Crossing his arms, Jack returned his gaze to the parking lot. White blotted out any remaining color, and the snow disguised the silver of her rental car. "I'm sure the company wouldn't be too pleased."

Molly tilted her chin upward and blinked her brown eyes. "Can she stay with us, Daddy? We have an extra bedroom."

"Molly." Jack spoke sharper than he intended. His daughter's wounded expression cut his emotions to the core, but how could he explain Sydney Ryan staying under his roof was not appropriate? He'd shared the house with Molly's mother. No other woman would ever take his late wife's place.

After Sydney shrugged on her jacket, she crouched in front of Molly again. "Thanks for thinking of me, Molly, but I'll keep my reservation. I enjoy staying in hotels, especially the old ones, which intrigue me. I imagine who else has stayed there, like who they were, what they did, and why they were there. Besides, I'd be in the way at your house. I don't want to interfere with you and your father's routine."

"You wouldn't be in the way. Promise." Molly turned. "Daddy, please make her come with us."

Sydney placed her hands on Molly's shoulders and squeezed. "I'll be fine, honey. I'm looking forward to checking out the Grand Hotel."

"How about dinner? You have to eat." Molly turned her attention back to the reality TV star.

His daughter displayed the stubborn trait she'd inherited from Jack. Now was not the time for her to dig her heels into the floor. Dinner was a bad idea. The more time he spent near Sydney Ryan, would make resisting her charm harder and detrimental to remaining firm about her not using Joe's Café as one of her projects. Molly would also be devastated when the reality TV star returned to L.A.

Sydney tugged on Molly's braid. "Tell you what. I'll stop in for breakfast tomorrow, and afterward you can show me how to make a snow angel. Your mother would like that."

With a ghost of a smile, she adjusted Molly's collar and brushed a piece of lint from his daughter's shoulder. The caring and intimate action pulled the breath from his lungs, and not in a good way, when he noticed his daughter's adoring look. At the mention of his late wife, Jack wondered what Molly said about her mother, but he realized Sydney only held compassion for his daughter. She must be another kindred spirit.

Dread curled around his heart. With luck, the snow would melt overnight so she couldn't make snow angels with Molly and assure Sydney would make it to Denver. He wouldn't change his mind.

Seeing her on television every week was one thing, but having her inside his restaurant was something else. Sweat gathered under his arms when he realized he wanted to reach out and touch her warmth. Jack wanted her to look at him like she did Molly, but that idea was a bad thing. He didn't need any other complications packaged up in Sydney Ryan.

****

"Let's walk Sydney Ryan to the hotel and get home before the storm gets worse, Molly." He leaned over to cup Sydney's elbow and helped her stand.

"That's unnecessary. I can drive across the street." Sydney swore she felt the warmth of his hand through her jacket. His touch confused her. On one hand, she sensed he wanted her gone, but on the other, he seemed not to want to let her out of his sight. Still, she appreciated his tenderness and caring toward her, and when he removed his hand, she felt lost. Jack's masculine scent toyed with her senses.

Ignoring her reaction to the man, Sydney focused on the task at hand. She'd return tomorrow. If she caved under every conflict and gave up without a fight, she wouldn't be a success today. Her producer required the episode, Sydney wanted her contract renewed, and Jack Ransom needed her help.

"I insist. It would take you longer to drive. You can pick up your car tomorrow."

At his deep tone, she didn't argue any further. He escorted her to the front door, opened it, and motioned for her to go down the steps. Cold hit her full force. Despite her newly purchased winter jacket, Sydney shivered. She should have bought mittens and a hat. How did people live in this cold? The moderate temperatures of L.A. seemed a distant memory. The Caymans would be a welcome break.

Sydney made it to the base of the porch, her boot-encased footsteps muffled by the layer of white. Snowflakes fell in a silent rhythm, blotting out the gray descending on the small town. More snow clung to the bare branches of the trees lining the street where someone hung Christmas lights. The tiny, white lights twinkled, adding another dimension to the coziness surrounding her as did the smell of burning wood drifting in the still air. Magical. Too bad she didn't buy into the romance.

Instead of watching Jack lean over the trunk for her suitcase, Sydney distracted herself by glancing at the garland and lights wrapped around the lamp posts complemented by red ribbons near the top. Along the third floor of the red brick hotel across the street, the staff placed more garland and red ribbons between the white, paned windows. "How quaint. Does Silver Ridge always do such an amazing job decorating for the holidays?" Sydney understood her bosses' request. This episode would hit at the core of the idolized, small-town America.

"Yes. We'll be decorating the restaurant next weekend. Christmas is our favorite time of the year." Jack smiled.

The pride in his voice for the town matched that for his shop. She didn't miss the loving look he gave his daughter. Sydney felt like an intruder watching the interaction.

"I wish you'd be here, Ms. Sydney." Molly tugged her sleeve; her eyes filled with moisture again.

Looking at Jack's precious daughter made her heart melt. If Sydney ever had children, she wanted one like Molly. "Take pictures and send them to me at the studio, and I'll be here in spirit."

"We'll be pen pals! That would be cool."

"We can. I'll rummage through our storeroom and find you a *Ryan to the Rescue* T-shirt."

Molly clapped and jumped. "Oh, Ms. Sydney, that would be amazing. I'd be the only kid in my class to have one."

"You'd be the only one in town, I'm sure." Sydney smiled at Jack's daughter again.

"I'll wear it at the Christmas Festival. Our town goes all out with luminaries and stuff. Even Santa takes time out of his schedule and comes to visit."

"Santa? No way." Sydney wished she believed in the magic of Christmas. Over the years, her cynicism grew, and she couldn't wait until the commercialism of the holiday season passed…until arriving here in Silver Ridge. Despite the snow and the cold, the town made her want to linger, or maybe Jack and his daughter made the difference.

"Yes, and his elves, too." Molly's eyes grew wide. "Sometimes, Mrs. Claus comes, but we never know until the festival. Are you sure you can't come back and join us?"

"I'm sure Ms. Ryan has better things to do, Molly." Jack growled.

The undercurrent in his words broke the stillness. Sydney couldn't leave soon enough for his liking.

Safely up the hotel's three stairs and under the green awning, the soft yellow light ended the intimacy. The man released her elbow, and she felt adrift in the sea of white surrounding her. Sydney stared, noticing the way his curly hair peeked out from underneath his hat and the five-o'clock shadow hugged his jawline. His eyes, hot as the flickering gas lamp on the wall, held fire as his gaze froze on her lips.

"Thanks for the escort. Good night, Molly. Mr. Ransom." Sydney stepped back and snatched her suitcase. She touched the cold metal handle on the old wood door, and with the flick of her wrist, opened it, and escaped into the welcoming interior before she did something stupid like kiss him.

****

"Daddy, we need her. We need Sydney Ryan's help." Molly grabbed her stuffed green elephant from her nightstand and jumped into bed.

Moisture welled in his daughter's eyes as she lay on her pillow. "No, we don't, Molly." Jack pulled up her purple and pink butterfly comforter. He touched her cheek. His love for Molly overwhelmed him. When Marin told him they were expecting, he hadn't understood how rewarding or challenging parenting would be. He also hadn't understood he'd do most of the parenting by himself. He looked at the ceiling and wondered if Marin watched them. Would she approve of his job with their daughter? What would she think of Molly writing the letter to Sydney Ryan? What would she think of the restaurant?

"Please, Daddy?" Molly whispered.

He refused to be swayed by his daughter's plea. "We can fix the place ourselves."

"But we watch her show every week. You always say she does a great job, and the other owners are happy she helped them. Why not us?"

He ignored Molly's quivering lip, and the way she clutched her bedspread and stared at her braid. Jack had no answer. Meeting Sydney Ryan caused an uneasy feeling he didn't want to acknowledge or explore. He sighed and kissed Molly's forehead. "Good night, honey. Tomorrow will be here before you know it."

Jack paced his small living room, clenching and unclenching his fists, keeping time with his footsteps. Molly finally settled after thirty minutes. All she talked about was Sydney Ryan and how her letter convinced the reality TV star to come to Silver Ridge.

"How could you, Uncle Ray?" Jack growled into

his cell phone a few minutes later. He stared at the picture of him, Marin, and a younger Molly having a picnic by the stream in the park outside of town. One of the last happy times they spent together before Marin got sick. He shut his eyes, willing the despair and anguish to subside.

"How could I what?"

"Don't play innocent." He circled the coffee table again, almost bumping his shin against the hard angle with the child guard still attached. "We go back way too far. Why did you encourage Molly to write to Sydney Ryan?"

Uncle Ray sighed. "The idea was Molly's. I got her the address and a stamp. Why is it such a bad thing?"

He clenched his fist again. "We can fix the place ourselves. Molly's infatuated. She wanted Sydney Ryan to spend the night here. She wants her to make snow angels after breakfast tomorrow."

"Is that so?"

Jack didn't appreciate the speculation in his uncle's voice. "Uncle Ray."

Silence. Jack suspected Uncle Ray's thoughts. Jack needed to move on from Marin's death and date again. He ran a finger along the outline of his late wife's face. His heart ached. Jack wasn't ready and didn't know if he ever would be.

****

"Good morning, Ryan. Just checking in."

Becca's voice floated over Sydney's cell phone Sunday morning. "Morning, Becca. You're up early." Sydney shifted in the queen-sized bed and rubbed the sleep from her eyes. She'd stayed up too late last night, watching old reruns on the television, trying to dislodge the thoughts of Jack and Molly. No matter which program she tried, she only saw images of the father, his daughter, and the letter. Sydney could help them. Getting Jack to change his mind had nothing to do with her new contract. Molly wanted her father to smile again, and Sydney had the power to make her wish happen.

Cradling the phone, she yawned and stretched her arms over her head. The lack of traffic noise, and the clang of the radiator kept her awake half the night, along with the firm mattress, and she'd forgotten to bring her pillow. She needed to wake up and think of another approach to get Jack to sign the contract.

"No rest for the wicked, or the weary. Tabitha's got the flu, so I've been up all night, and I'm not feeling great either."

"Sorry to hear that. I hope you both get well soon." Sydney kicked off the patterned, cream-colored bedspread. The blackout curtains did their job, and she'd forgotten to set her phone alarm.

"Tabitha will get over hers a lot quicker. I'm pregnant again."

Her producer's condition explained a lot of things. Sydney smiled, remembering how disorganized and tired her producer was for the last couple of weeks. "Congratulations! I'm so happy for all of you." Children were a blessing. Molly's image rose in her mind's eye. "A boy or a girl?"

"Thanks. I think the baby's another girl. I should buy stock in soda crackers. The morning sickness is awful."

"I'm sorry. Let me know what I can do for you."

"Get me a signed contract. So, all chatting aside,

how's it going? Don't mess with a pregnant lady and evade the question again."

"Yes, ma'am. Things are okay." Sydney climbed from the bed and padded across the maroon and gold carpet to the window. She pulled back the heavy, brown curtains, revealing white lace sheers underneath. After pushing aside those, she stared at the sea of white. Not much stirred at six-fifteen in the morning, and snowfall hushed all sounds. A strip of black pavement between the hotel and the café created a straight line between the tree-lined area. She wondered how much snow had fallen. "I arrived ahead of a blizzard. Everything's so white here, and cold."

"That happens in parts of our country. I haven't had a white Christmas since I left Minnesota."

"You can have it. I'll take the Caymans." Sydney shivered, remembering the wind's bitter chill while walking across the street with Jack and Molly Ransom. She refused to think about her reaction when he held her arm. She had no time for romance.

"Hmmm. Cold, snow, and dead car batteries. Don't miss it at all. Have you discovered who wrote the letter?"

Her producer was relentless, but that quality is what made Becca successful. Sydney let her gaze linger on the old train depot. She needed coffee. "Yes. I've run into one complication."

"I didn't hear that word. Nothing is better than airing a Christmastime special in a snowy place. A small, cozy town nestled in the heart of the Rockies. I'm envisioning the opening scene with the little girl reading her letter. We'll have the snow in the background and a roaring fire and Christmas lights.

This episode will differ from what we've done before, and it will tug at the heartstrings of middle America. Bring goodwill toward men complete with all the holiday trappings. We need this restaurant for your show. Ratings, Sydney."

She hated that word, but her contract depended on ratings. Was Sydney doing a disservice to her viewers by going along with the fake illusion? Sydney didn't like the thought she might be selling herself to the commercialism of Christmas. "You and Wilson did your homework."

"We always do. That's our job. So, what have you found out?"

Sydney rubbed her eyes again. "The owner wasn't pleased when he discovered his daughter wrote the letter."

"Ryan, we need this Christmas special, or Wilson will have both our heads on a platter. I need this job. I'll have another mouth to feed in seven months. Work your magic. You can convince anyone to do anything."

In the dim light cast from the streetlight, Sydney saw movement.

A man wearing a dark jacket carrying a shovel walked from behind the depot.

Jack. She'd recognized his broad shoulders and unruly hair sticking out from beneath his brown cap. When he looked between the rental car and the hotel, she let the curtain drop and stepped back. He couldn't see her, but she felt guilty about spying.

"I'll attempt again this morning. From what I saw yesterday, both the exterior and the interior need major work. The old building has charm, but the trim, the door, and clapboard siding need a fresh coat of paint.

Not sure if any exterior work will happen in this weather."

"We can try. What else?"

As Sydney paced the room, she caught sight of a plain envelope slipped under the door. Her brows furrowed as she strode across the carpet. Odd, she never received a bill until she checked out. Sydney pulled out the piece of paper.

The best time to eat at Joe's Café today is before 7:30.

The note had no signature, but Sydney got the message. Excitement coursed through her about the improvements she could make. Wilson and Becca were right. Joe's Café was a prime example of the place she *would* use for her show. "The restaurant needs a total makeover, from the faded exterior to the seventies décor. I'm sure the menu is outdated, too. The project is big."

"You've had bigger ones. Get permission from the owner. No pressure, but remember, the crew arrives next Saturday."

Tick tock. Each breath brought her closer to the weekend. Butterflies took flight in her stomach. She had to find a way to get Jack to say yes.

****

Fresh-brewed coffee teased her nostrils when Sydney entered Joe's Café thirty minutes later. She could almost taste her first cup. A strong dose of caffeine would help her plan her next offense in getting Jack's agreement.

"Good morning, Ms. Sydney. You came like you said you would! Look, my hair is still braided."

Grinning, Molly ran from behind the counter and

wrapped her arms around her waist. "Yes, I did." Sydney smiled as she patted down a few strays. At least the girl looked happy to see her, contrasting with the frown pursing Jack's lips.

"Good morning, Ms. Ryan."

Sydney took his lead as she sat at the counter. "Good morning, Mr. Ransom. May I have coffee with cream and sugar, please?"

"Of course." Jack turned over a cup and poured the dark liquid.

She picked up a laminated menu to avoid staring at the man with the dark, curly hair in need of a trim. He had blue eyes like the color of the Pacific Ocean on a sunny summer day. A five o'clock shadow hugged his rugged cheeks and chin and a blue-and-white-checkered flannel shirt clung to his broad shoulders. She wasn't attracted, but his nearness made breathing impossible.

Reading the outdated menu was a safer option. Combinations of eggs, meats, potatoes, and breads along with standard drink items. No healthy options to attract the upscale population moving into Silver Ridge. Her producer wasn't the only one who completed her homework. The antique cuckoo clock behind the counter sounded seven times. Valuable time slipped away. She should be making notes and thinking up new menu items, not wasting another moment convincing him to do the right thing. "Have you reconsidered my offer?"

"No. Don't ask again."

His dark expression only added to the frustration nipping her consciousness. Her contract was on the line, along with Jack's and Molly's futures. Why couldn't he accept what she had to offer "I can turn this place into a gold mine like I've done with a hundred other restaurants, Mr. Ransom." She gripped the edge of the worn counter. "I'm not leaving until you've signed the contract."

****

"Then I guess you should find a cheaper place to stay. You'll be here a long time." Jack clenched his jaw. Why did he vocalize his thoughts? He wanted her gone, not hanging around influencing his daughter or wearing down his defenses.

"That's a good idea. Do you have a place in mind?"

Her smile lit her face and created havoc with the coffee he'd drunk earlier. Shouldn't she still be on L.A. time? Shouldn't she still be asleep? Shouldn't he stop thinking about Sydney Ryan's sleeping arrangements?

"Here." Jack growled and pushed the ceramic cup and a ramekin full of different sweeteners toward her instead of taking any chance of an incidental contact. Sydney bothered him and made him uncomfortable. He needed to think about increasing business himself, not be distracted by the reality TV star his daughter idolized and convinced to come to town.

His family had owned the restaurant too long to fail, but Sydney Ryan's help wasn't an option. He would not expose his daughter or his staff to the world by putting them on television. His pride would not accept charity handouts, and if Marin were still alive, her pride wouldn't either. They'd had their own vision for the place, and letting a stranger make changes wasn't right. He still felt Marin's presence inside. Changing things could alter his feelings.

Sure, Joe's Café had faded over time, but his

31

restaurant wasn't like the other places Sydney rescued. He made sure to rotate his limited stock and keep the place clean. His few employees were helpful and friendly, and he had decent standards for the food that left his kitchen. Very few meals were sent back, and his last health inspection netted a high score. He just needed more customers. "Would you like to place an order?"

"No, thanks."

Jack's emotions flipped between relief and anger the chef-turned-restaurant-rescuer refused to eat his food. The simple fare he created satisfied everyone else who walked through his front door. "One ninety-five then."

Sydney placed three dollars on the counter and then picked up her drink.

Out of the corner of his eye, he watched the gentle sway of her hips as she wandered to the table where he'd first seen her yesterday. The subtle scent of berries lingered in the air and teased his senses. The camera and clothing she wore on *Ryan to the Rescue* hid her womanly curves.

He rubbed the stubble on his cheek and dragged his gaze to the scenery beyond the front window. Sunrise stained the area gray. If he walked outside to the back and looked at the snowy mountains, he'd see the purple streaks stretching across the sky pushing away the darkness. Orange, then yellow would follow before the sky crystallized into blue. A chill ran through him, and a few moments later, Jack put another log in the fire. More warmth spilled from the large opening, but the feeling wouldn't recede until he'd seen the last of Sydney Ryan.

The bell jingled over the door.

Jack turned and watched an elderly couple walk in. He rose from his haunches. "Good morning, Mr. and Mrs. Johnson. Welcome to Joe's Café." Jack hadn't seen his neighbors or the Westins inside the restaurant in months. Why of all days did they show up when half his staff called in late or sick? He glanced at Sydney looking around the interior of the restaurant. No. Couldn't be. She wouldn't stoop so low, would she?

Chapter Three

Sydney liked the personal touch. She sipped and let the coffee linger, watching Jack as he retrieved menus for the couple sitting at the other window table. He made a great cup of coffee. She looked at the girl who followed her from the counter. "Have a seat, Molly. You've seen my show. What would you do here?"

Molly sat in the opposite chair. "I'd paint the inside in really cool colors, and make the tables easier to wash, and make yummy milkshakes. Everyone loves milkshakes. When I take over, I'll serve milkshakes, chicken nuggets, and macaroni and cheese."

All typical items on a children's menu. Sydney smiled and made a mental note to create a children's section on her new menu once she had Jack's approval to do the makeover. She had no time to waste if she wanted to see the Cayman Islands for Christmas.

She glanced around the room again. A time warp dated this place to the seventies. The potential to be quaint and cozy settled in the mediocre. Her makeover would bring in customers, but her time ran short. Jack had to agree to let her work her magic to save his café and assure her a new contract with a raise, so she could put away more money to fund her dream of owning her own restaurant.

"You're right. Everyone loves a good milkshake. What's your favorite flavor? Mine's chocolate."

Sydney swallowed the rest of her words with another sip. With the lack of customers yesterday, Molly would have nothing to take over unless Sydney helped. More determination set in. The paperwork remained inside her bag on the table. Jack would say yes.

The bell above the door jingled again.

"We're having an early rush, Molly. Please seat Mr. and Mrs. Peterson and pour them two coffees." Jack pulled out a pen and a pad of paper from his white apron and approached the first couple.

Molly jumped from her seat. "Mine's chocolate, too. Okay, Daddy. Mrs. Collins is sick so I'm helping. Uncle Ray doesn't work on Sundays, and our cook is late. Daddy won't let me help in the kitchen yet, but I can when I'm ten. I've got a lot to learn for the business, you know."

The confidence slid from Molly's expression and wistful hope sprung in her eyes.

"Will you still be here, Ms. Sydney? You promised we'd make snow angels. Please?"

Sydney smiled again at Molly's choice of words. She sounded more grown-up than certain people Sydney knew. Molly's maturity didn't surprise her because she spent a lot of time around adults in the restaurant. Sydney looked at Jack. She wasn't leaving. "I will be."

His closed expression told her he wouldn't relax until she left Silver Ridge. Beneath the soothing scent of coffee and the crackle and snap of the fire in the fireplace, tension settled in her muscles. She took another drink and watched Molly tie a white apron around her waist. Then she poured two cups of coffee and loaded them on a tray with a small pitcher of cream and a ramekin of assorted sweeteners.

The thud of a closing car door caught her attention. Jack's, too. A party of six walked inside, and his expression morphed from closed to harried to resigned.

Another car pulled into the lot.

Sydney thought about the message she'd received earlier, and the knowledge one of his employees was sick and the other ran late. Coincidence or conspiracy? She smiled. Jack and Molly appeared to be the only staff, so whoever wrote the note knew about her background and wanted to make sure she had plenty of time to change Jack's mind.

Still grinning, Sydney pulled the emergency elastic band from her purse and twisted her hair into a serviceable ponytail. Then she pushed back her chair and cleared her table. "Welcome to Joe's Café, folks. We'll be right with you." She strode to the counter.

"What are you doing?" Jack hissed. He shoved the pen behind his ear and met her by the cash register.

Sydney spied the bus tub on a three-shelf utility cart and set her cup inside. Adrenaline and the initial caffeine buzz should keep her going for a while. "I need an apron. Where do you keep them?" Unperturbed, Sydney looked under the counter where Molly retrieved hers earlier. She only saw a stack of towels, extra silverware, napkins, and condiments.

"I'm not letting you do anything here." He folded his arms, blocking her path.

"An apron, Mr. Ransom." She stepped past him and crouched.

The bells jingled again.

"I don't see you've got a choice. Do you believe Molly can handle this crowd by herself?" She pushed the towels to the side and saw a well-worn apron at the back. Ten seconds later, she tied the apron around her waist, defying Jack. No one intimidated her in or out of the kitchen, not even renowned and antagonistic Chef Bruno who taught her everything. "Do you have a cook this morning?"

Jack closed his eyes and pursed his lips. "You're looking at him until Frank comes in."

Behind them, Sydney heard Molly pull two tables together for the six-top as a hum of voices filled the space. "Then I'm glad I'm here." She itched to get on the floor and help his daughter. The sooner she got people situated, the better. Working in the front of the house would help her solidify all the changes needed once she got permission to work her magic.

"Have you ever waited tables?"

His last-ditch effort to throw her off failed. She held his gaze. "I have, but does my experience matter on Thanksgiving weekend? No one wants to cook with their family in town."

"Here." He ripped off the latest order and held out the pad and pen. "Watch Molly so she doesn't hurt herself. This idea is crazy. *The* Sydney Ryan waiting tables at Joe's Café."

"I got dressed this morning like everyone else who has walked through the front door. Now go." Sydney shooed Jack toward the kitchen. She stepped out on the floor determined to use these hours to her advantage. Seven hours with Jack should give her plenty of time to wear down his defenses.

****

Mid-morning, Sydney brushed against Jack as she stepped behind the line to help plate the order for another party of six. Heat flushed her cheeks that had nothing to do with the temperature inside the cramped area. "If you opened this space a few inches, we wouldn't be bumping into each other."

Jack plated two pancakes. "Nice try. The kitchen has worked this way for fifty years; it'll work for another fifty." He handed her the plate. "This order needs bacon and those scrambled eggs."

Sydney widened her eyes as she accepted it, making certain to avoid contact. A few moments earlier heightened her awareness enough for her to register she wasn't immune to his rugged charm. "I can't serve food on this plate."

"What's wrong?" Jack wiped his brow with the sleeve of his T-shirt.

"The plate's chipped."

He shrugged and turned his attention back to the eggs on the grill. "Most of them are. The customers don't mind. Bacon, please? You're delaying the order."

"Yes, I am." Sydney marched to the trash can and dumped the plate inside.

"Hey, that was good food." Jack growled.

His anger didn't bother her. She'd faced worse while learning the trade. She stomped back; her voice seething as her finger drilled into his chest. "You have a roomful of customers expecting a high level of quality from the food to the plate." Several people also recognized her, so what she put on the table was a reflection on her, too. "Max, pull all the chipped plates and throw them in the garbage can."

"Yes, ma'am."

The tall, thin, dark-haired teenager who doubled as dishwasher and busboy placed his hand over his mouth and covered his laughter.

A heartbeat later, she caught Jack furrowing his eyebrows as his lips formed a straight line. His eyes cooled, which only made her more determined to get him to agree.

"Max, do not do as the lady says. Put them on the back shelf, for today."

Sydney won a small victory. With a little more work, the bigger one was within her grasp.

****

At two o'clock, Jack emerged from the kitchen carrying three plates filled with scrambled eggs, sausage, and wheat toast. "Let's eat." He sank onto the chair next to his daughter and across from Sydney. Mistake. From this vantage point, he saw the soft curve of her neck, the fullness of her lips, and watched her eyes sparkle when she looked at Molly. Maybe he should have sat beside her, but then he'd want to reach out to touch her warmth.

He did not understand the spell she cast. Each time she entered the kitchen, he tracked her to the point of distraction. Two, over-easy eggs wound up over-hard, and he'd burnt six pieces of toast. He felt like an amateur when she made a complicated, special-order omelet, and the other times she stepped behind the line.

Even when she threw away good food, his anger dissipated in minutes. He wished he shared her passion. He had it once and buried it three years ago.

Sweat formed under his arms as he remembered the few times their hands connected and made him forget his promise to Marin. No one would take his late wife's place. Not even Sydney Ryan, who would be on her way back to L.A. by early evening if he had his way.

"Thanks for breakfast." Sydney tucked her napkin onto her lap.

"You're welcome." Would she eat his food now? She had to be hungry after working half the day.

"Thank goodness you were here, Ms. Sydney. How did you know what to do? I thought you just fixed places." Molly bit into a piece of toast, her eyes wide, as she stared.

"I put myself through school waiting tables. Once you learn, you never forget. Plus, I had an excellent coworker who helped and kept me in line." Sydney tweaked Molly's nose.

The reality TV star's smile lit up her face, pulling the breath from his lungs. When Molly giggled and gazed longingly at Sydney, Jack forced himself not to do the same. "You know your way around the kitchen, too." His stomach growled as he smeared his toast with strawberry jelly. The restaurant hadn't been this busy in a while, so he'd only grabbed an occasional drink. Being short-staffed didn't help either. Frank called in sick, and when Max came in at eight, they barely kept up. Coincidence or conspiracy?

Sydney toyed with her eggs. "As you can see, I've done my time behind the line, too. That's why my show's a success."

He focused on her plate, or he'd forget all the reasons he shouldn't look at her or forget the real reason for her being here. "You don't like your food."

"I do. See?" She scooped eggs into her mouth.

All Jack saw was how she held her fork and the elegant way she dabbed the napkin against her lips. He bit off a piece of toast and chewed, although the bread tasted like sawdust. "Where did you learn?"

Her chin rose a fraction. "I went to the San Diego Culinary Institute. From there I found a job at the Blue Seas Resort in Orange County for four years, and then at their sister property in L.A. for three more. Then I won a cooking competition and got an internship with infamous Chef Charles Bruno. When he retired, I landed my own contract and created *Ryan to the Rescue*." Sydney smiled at Molly.

He wished she'd smile in his direction. No. Tiredness crept in. The woman spelled trouble, and the silky smoothness of her voice reminded him of what was missing in his life. She needed to leave Silver Ridge so he could still his mind and focus on what mattered. Molly and his café.

"And now you're here."

Jack didn't like Molly's expression, and if he wasn't mistaken, she winked. No. He remained firm. Sydney would not use Joe's Café for her show. Even though she fit inside his restaurant, and he and Marin *had* thought about updating the kitchen, he'd figure out how to save his family legacy.

"Yes, I'm here." Sydney pulled the stack of bills from her apron pocket and pushed them toward Molly. "These tips are for you."

"Not so fast. You earned the money." Jack failed to remove the censure from his tone, just as he floundered keeping pace with the orders without her help.

"I don't want the tips. Put it in a college fund for Molly so she can go to culinary school if she wants, or better yet, buy new plates."

Molly crossed her arms and pursed her lips. "New plates would be nice, Daddy, because our customers deserve the best."

"Our customers already have the best." Jack didn't appreciate the woman encouraging his daughter to push her agenda. It didn't matter Molly contacted the woman. He'd given Sydney Ryan his answer twice, and he would not change his mind. "Let's clean up. Morgan's birthday party starts at four thirty."

"Okay, Daddy." Molly tugged on Sydney's sleeve. "Will you let me show you how to make a snow angel before you go, Ms. Sydney?"

Jack clenched his jaw. He wanted the reality television star out of Silver Ridge, not butting in where she didn't belong, and usurping the memories of Marin.

****

Molly's plea tugged at Sydney's heart. The girl missed her mother, and she couldn't blame her. Judging from yesterday and today, the café consumed Jack, and he didn't have much time left over for his daughter. He would have plenty of hours if Jack let her help.

"Ms. Ryan has things to do, Molly, and so do we." Jack dropped his napkin on his empty plate.

Sydney understood what Jack didn't say–Go away and leave us alone.

He pushed back his chair, stood, and then cupped his daughter's shoulders. "I'll make one with you once we're done here, I promise."

Moisture filled Molly's eyes, and she jutted out her bottom lip.

Her expression created another wave of sympathy. Jack would miss another opportunity to spend precious time with his daughter. Clean-up would always be there, but Molly would grow up and start her own life in the blink of an eye.

Molly's shoulders slumped. "That's what you always say."

"I'd love you to. Let's clean up, and then you can show me what to do." Sydney knew she overstepped her bounds, but she chose Molly's side. She squeezed the girl's hand. She made a promise yesterday, and she always kept her promises, especially the one to Becca. The longer she worked on Jack, the better. She wouldn't leave until she filmed her episode. Jack needed to understand his best interests were to let her work her magic. If she didn't, she might as well not even return to L.A.

Outside in the fresh snow, Sydney sat, lay next to Molly, and moved her arms and legs. She stared at the deep blue sky. Cold penetrated her wool jacket, but Sydney didn't mind. She'd seen children make snow angels in the movies but never experienced the activity. She smiled. Memories of her mother and Sydney making sandcastles on Santa Monica Beach flashed in her mind's eye. Had Molly ever seen the ocean?

Aside from creating the legacy for Jack to pass onto his daughter, Sydney would love to give Molly a beach experience and many others. In the brief time she'd known her, she couldn't deny that the girl wormed her way into Sydney's heart. Maybe she'd invite Jack and Molly out to L.A. the next time she renovated a local restaurant.

Sydney returned Molly's smile with one of her own. She didn't know what Molly's mom looked like, but she imagined a grown-up version of the girl gazing from Heaven. Despite her aching heart, Sydney grinned. She understood the loneliness, the isolation, although she wondered if she projected her thoughts.

Except for needing extra attention, Molly seemed well enough adjusted.

After she studied their handiwork, Sydney brushed the snow from Molly's back, then Molly did hers in return. The action seemed so normal, as if it happened every day.

"That was fun. Can we build a snowman next?"

Sydney shoved her thoughts back into the recesses of her mind. "Sure, sweetie." The endearment slipped from her lips, and Sydney saw longing flicker across Molly's face. "I've never made one of those before either. I need you to show me how."

"Okay. First you make a snowball and then you roll it." Molly knelt and gathered snow in her gloved hands. "Packing snow is the best." She rolled the ball in the snow. "I'll make the head if you make the middle. We can do the bottom together."

"That sounds like a plan." Sydney mimicked Molly and wished again that she'd brought gloves. Cold burned her palms and fingers, but the sensation was just temporary. Excitement filled her, and she felt childlike again with no cares in the world, no producer phone calls filling her voicemail, and no future contract negotiations.

A wet snowball hit the ground beside her. "Hey, Molly, why did you do that?"

"Do what?"

Sydney shifted her gaze and saw Molly kneeling in the snow a few feet from her, making her own ball. If Molly hadn't thrown…Sydney turned toward the direction of the snowball.

Jack snuck behind them, readying another snowball in his gloved hands.

A crooked grin transformed his lips. "No fair sneaking up on us poor defenseless women."

Molly giggled. "You're in trouble now, Daddy."

"I doubt you're defenseless, Ms. Ryan." Jack tossed the snowball between his hands.

"That's right." Sydney hurled her snowball at Jack. She'd never experienced a snowball fight, but she was well aware of them. Plus, she had throwing experience. She gathered more snow.

"Snowball fight." Molly threw a snowball at her dad, then one at Sydney.

Sydney leapt backward moments before Jack's snowball sailed by her shoulder. She sensed more to this game than he led on. He fought her being there, having his reasons for her to leave. She had her reasons to stay.

In an instant, she realized her being here wasn't about her show or her future contract. She wouldn't leave until Jack had a legacy to leave to Molly.

After kneeling behind the tree, she formed several snowballs in rapid succession. She lobbed a few soft ones at Molly, who now stood by her father, an enormous grin splitting her red face. Then she focused her attention on the man using the porch railing as protection. She wasn't as gentle. This time she displaced his cap. The next smacked his knee. She wound another pitch as a snowball dropped beside her.

"Uncle. I give." Jack raised his hands. He stood and made quick work of the distance until he stood mere inches away, with Molly at his heels.

She brushed the snow from his jacket. He stilled her hand, his touch bringing her warmth. His five o'clock shadow stood out against the white backdrop, and butterflies wreaked havoc in her stomach. What was happening? She was too old for a schoolgirl crush.

After Jack brushed the remaining snow from his jacket, he folded his arms, his half grin sliding across his face.

A new appreciation filled his eyes. "We needed you on our baseball team. I couldn't catch anything the pitcher threw, and we lost every game."

"Sorry about that." And she was.

"You were awesome, Ms. Sydney. Can we make a snowman now?"

Sydney knelt and straightened Molly's coat collar. "Thanks. Sure. Unless your father needs you. Mr. Ransom?"

Jack straightened his cap and adjusted his gloves. "I came to see if you needed help."

Molly squealed and clapped her hands. "We do, Daddy. I'm making the head, Ms. Sydney's making the middle, so you can make the bottom."

Sydney stood and placed a hand on her chest to still her heart's rapid beat. She retreated a few feet, glad her presence made Jack stop working and spend time with his daughter. His being there also gave her another opportunity to get him to change his mind, but his nearness left her out of sorts.

"Leaving before your work is finished? That's not the Sydney Ryan you portray on your show." Jack's fisted hands on his waist matched the challenge in his expression.

"Not at all." Sydney held his gaze. Her take-no-prisoner attitude won her the contest, allowing her to work with the industry's best. Her training with Chef Bruno led to her show's success. She wouldn't leave now, despite the crazy emotions erupting inside.

Jack moved nearby. "I would have never guessed you could throw like a professional."

"I keep my personal and professional lives separate." She inched backward again. Distance. She needed more room so she could think. "I don't need that skill to renovate a restaurant."

"True. But where did you learn?" Jack decreased the space between them.

"My father."

Jack stepped to his right and leaned against the tree. "He taught you well. Are you close?"

Sydney stiffened. "I haven't seen him since my high school graduation, but I learned he died a few years ago." She didn't speak about her father, but Jack drew out things she'd never shared with anyone else. She refused to stop and examine the meaning, because then she'd have to admit she'd started to have feelings for Jack and his daughter.

His expression softened. "I'm sorry. And your mother?"

Sydney looked at Molly. "I was eight when she died in a car accident."

"I'm sorry about that, too."

Compassion filled Jack's voice, but Sydney didn't want his pity. She'd had enough to last a lifetime. Things happened. Life wasn't fair. Each time she discovered someone else who'd lost their mother, especially children, it reopened unhealed wounds.

Perhaps that was why Sydney buried herself in work. She spent her time fixing things to avoid fixing herself. She dodged holiday invitations to escape the reminder of her dysfunctional childhood. If she failed to get Jack's agreement, coming to Silver Ridge during the holidays with the lights, and the decorations, and the Christmas magic was a mistake.

"I'm that old now. So, you don't have a mother, like me. I knew you were special." Molly wrapped her arms around Sydney's waist and leaned against her, burying her face in Sydney's gray-and-black houndstooth coat.

Instinctively, she hugged the child. "And you, too. We're two peas in a pod and belong to a special club. No matter what happens, we'll always have that bond." Sydney bit her lip. Her heart ached at the natural motherly instinct. Kneeling, she gathered Molly in her arms, drinking in her warmth as she rubbed her cheek against her beanie.

Jack's daughter clung, her thin body trembling.

Sydney related to Molly's loneliness. She glanced at Jack, and a whirl of butterflies took flight again. He looked just as lost and lonely. His unkempt hair, five o'clock shadow, and a crooked smile affected her. She swallowed.

Focus on your job, Sydney, not the owner. She shifted her attention to the train depot, her critical eye scanning the exterior. She didn't have Jack's permission yet, but she would. She'd create ideas in her room later for the fresh look inside and out, and the new kitchen, and menu items.

"I love you, Ms. Sydney. You're kind, caring, and smart. You do amazing things with other people's restaurants and know how to braid hair. You'd make a good mommy."

"Thank you, Molly. Those words mean a lot." She squeezed tighter, imprinting the feel of holding her long after Silver Ridge was nothing but a successful episode and a warm, distant memory.

"You're welcome. I wish you could help us. I think my mommy would have liked that."

Feeling Molly tremble, Sydney knew tears spilled down her cheeks. She extracted herself from Molly's grasp and wiped away the moisture with the pads of her thumbs. With six more days until the crew arrived, Sydney still had so much to accomplish. "I do, too, but unless your father changes his mind, I can't."

"I won't, Ms. Ryan, so quit asking."

Three no's. Tick tock. The clock hands spun closer to Saturday. Sydney had until end of business Friday to get Jack to agree, or she'd need to tell Becca to cancel the crew's travel arrangements. Sydney never experienced this much trouble, but then again, the owner normally contacted the network, not his daughter without his knowledge.

"I will when you agree. I'll be back tomorrow." Sydney squared her shoulders. Quitters got nowhere.

****

"Daddy? Was my mommy a good mommy? I don't remember." Molly stomped in the fresh layer of snow.

As Jack locked the back door at three thirty, he swallowed. Molly was three when Marin got sick, and she died two months before her fifth birthday. Outside of pictures, his daughter had no memory of her mother besides what Jack and her other grandparents told her. Each day he struggled to remember his late wife's smile, touch, wit, and wisdom. Daily problems crowded out the memories until they blurred, but he would always hear her last words.

"Take care of our Molly, Jacky, and take care of

yourself. Be happy. Love again."

Jack vowed he'd never fall in love again, and he'd honor his marriage vows even after the death-do-us-part happened. He tucked a stray piece of hair behind Molly's ear. He'd do anything to protect and care for her. Well, almost. Anything but allow Sydney Ryan to exploit his family and employees. "Your mom was the best. No one can take her place."

But was that comment for Molly's benefit, or his own?

Chapter Four

As Sydney walked across the hotel lobby later that afternoon, she watched a woman in her mid-sixties sporting a brunette bob and dressed in a bright red dress approach.

"We're honored you're staying with us." She smiled and held out a hand. "Hi, Sydney Ryan, I'm Cynthia Langley. My husband, Larry, and I own the hotel and restaurant. Welcome."

"Pleased to meet you, Cynthia. Your place is beautiful." Sydney accepted her proffered hand, her lips curving upward in return.

Cynthia shook her hand, her smiling widening, causing laugh lines around her warm, dark eyes. "Thank you, and the pleasure is mine. What brings you to town? To be honest, I'm starstruck. We don't get many celebrities here. They usually continue up the road to the ski resorts in Summit Falls."

"I got the nicest letter from Mary-Katerina Quinn."

A warm familiarity crossed Cynthia's face.

"Molly! She's such an amazing child." Then her smile disappeared, and frown lines gathered on her forehead. "It's such a—never mind. Please help yourself to refreshments, and then if you'd like, I'll give you a tour."

"I'd love a personalized tour." Sydney wondered what Cynthia left unsaid as she walked across the red, brown, and gold, patterned carpet covering the original tile flooring, but Jack's personal life was none of her business. At the rustic wood table next to the front desk, she grabbed a cup of chilled water infused with apples and cinnamon from the dainty dispenser.

Tan, stacked stones covered the wall, and the antique miner's lanterns hanging from wrought-iron hooks lit the gold and brown, Italian, faux-painted walls, casting a warm glow. Quaint. A potted fern planted inside a replica of an old ore cart sat next to a plate of frosted sugar cookies. Sydney grabbed an angel-shaped one and bit into its sweetness, thinking of Molly. The girl wormed her way inside her heart, and she wouldn't give up. "Whoever designed your décor did an amazing job."

"I did. Thanks. Coming from you, that's a genuine compliment. So, the office is to the right of the reception desk, and this is the lobby."

Sydney noticed the door with the wreath before she turned to look across the cozy area. Coffered wood beams stretched across the ceiling, cutting the large, off-white expanse into intimate sections. As she walked to the roaring fire in the old stone fireplace dominating the back of the lobby, Sydney noticed more mining equipment hanging on the walls.

"My husband's great-great-grandfather built the Grand Hotel in 1886."

She heard the pride in Cynthia's voice. "I'm so glad you kept it in the family. Sometimes the upkeep is too much, and many of these places sell out to corporations." The fire's warmth heated her chilled hands, while the aroma of burning wood, mingling with fresh pine, filled her nostrils.

Cynthia shrugged. "We've had trying times, and several offers, but Larry and I love it here and can't imagine doing anything else. Our son doesn't feel the same way, chose a law degree, and works for a Denver firm."

"Let's hope when you're ready to retire, he'll reconsider and return." Sydney stared at the garland intertwined with lights, gold ornaments, and red ribbons draped over the wood mantel. Something similar would work over the fireplace mantel at Joe's Café.

"Perhaps. When you're ready, we'll continue to the ballroom."

"I'm all set, thanks." Sydney didn't want to consume too much of her time. She stepped past the Christmas tree decorated with red poinsettias, green and red ribbons, and silver ornaments. The decorator interspersed more poinsettias among the presents and lobby, completing the festive mood. Additional lights and garland lit the six wooden posts holding up the ceiling. Two beautiful, stained-glass lamps hung in the main hallway that led to the elevators. Green garland, silver ornaments, and red ribbon graced each doorway on both sides of the hall.

Cynthia stopped in front of the ornate double doors and pushed the right one. "This is the Grand Ballroom. It isn't used as often anymore, but we hold a fair share of weddings and other parties. My husband told me stories of all the galas and events that happened here when he was a kid. This hotel was the only place in town for gatherings and community events." Cynthia flipped the light switch.

Sydney stepped into the interior, not knowing where to look first. More holiday decorations outlined the tall windows lining the far wall along with another Christmas tree decorated like the one in the lobby. Rich, brown wood paneling lined the walls, while stamped copper tiles covered the ceiling between the dark wood beams. Several elaborate chandeliers pushed away the late afternoon darkness. Numerous wood tables and chairs on the white marble floor invited guests to sit and stay. "I can imagine. The room is beautiful. I wouldn't change a thing." Sydney stepped outside.

Cynthia's smile chased away the lines creasing her forehead. "Thank you." Her hostess turned off the lights and shut the doors.

An old, black-and-white photograph hung on the wall to Sydney's left caught her attention. The plaque at the bottom read The Grand Hotel circa 1892.

"That photo was taken a few years after the hotel opened. There are several more photos along the wall if you want to look. Silver Ridge has its own historical museum a few blocks away with a lot more of the town's history. In fact, a fundraiser will be held there Monday night if you're interested. I'm providing the appetizers and could always use a second opinion."

"I'd like to visit there and would be happy to help." Sydney smiled and continued along the hallway. "Everything is so different here than where I grew up in L.A. I'm glad I came."

"We are, too. Molly's letter worked."

Surprise filled Sydney, and she pulled her attention from the photo to stare at her hostess. "You knew about the letter, too?"

The woman swatted the air. "Of course. My cousin, Suzette Collins, who works at Joe's Café, told me." She drew her lips together in a straight line. "But since you're here, and not across the street, that means Jack hasn't agreed to the makeover."

A sigh escaped. "He hasn't, and the production crew arrives next weekend."

"Well, Larry and I are glad you're here. Thanks to you and your staff, the hotel is almost full at one of our slowest times. That boy can be so pigheaded. His café isn't the only business suffering. Having you showcase our humble town would benefit us all."

Sydney looked at another old photograph of the hotel's rear entrance. In the background, she saw the train depot's corner. She looked back at Cynthia. "If I don't convince him to agree to the production, this season could be the end of *Ryan to the Rescue*."

Her hostess widened her eyes and gasped. "Oh, no. Everyone I know watches your show. We've got to figure out a way to change his mind."

"Let me know if you can think of one. Otherwise I'll need an alternative, or my name will be mud with my producer. Jack's refusal is a first." Sydney pursed her lips. "Most owners jump at the chance to have me come in and fix their restaurant."

"Most owners aren't like Jack. He changed when Marin died." Cynthia led her to one of the open doors across the hall.

Another wave of sorrow formed in the pit of her stomach. "I can imagine how hard being a single dad is for him, and for Molly."

"It hasn't been easy. Jack and Marin knew each other since first grade." She shook her head. "This is the Mother Lode room. On the weekends, we serve afternoon tea here. We're having a room full of young ladies for a birthday party later today."

The room was a mini version of the ballroom, complete with Christmas décor, too. White tablecloths sprinkled with silver and green confetti, red napkins, and delicate white china covered all ten tables. Each table contained a three-tiered silver plate standing ready for what Sydney guessed would be traditional tea food like petit fours, scones and jam, and finger sandwiches. On a long table at the back, a variety of old-fashioned hats waited for the birthday guests. "How sweet." She thought of Molly, knowing she'd enjoy this type of party. Sydney had never attended an afternoon tea, even though she'd prepared the food several times. Would Jack let her bring his daughter here next weekend?

Cynthia motioned Sydney out into the hall. "This next room has more photographs of the hotel and doubles as our gift shop in case you want to take back a souvenir. And finally, our business office if you need to copy or fax something."

Sydney looked to the right of the old phone booth and saw a few desks with computers and a large copier in the back. She suspected this area had once been part of the gift shop and was partitioned off to accommodate the business traveler. "Thanks, that offer might come in handy."

"Something you said earlier gave me an idea, Sydney."

In the lobby, Cynthia stopped short and placed a hand on Sydney's arm.

When Sydney faced her, she saw the hesitation written in the woman's eyes.

"If Jack doesn't agree, would you consider using our restaurant? The Piñon Gulch isn't as bad as the train depot, but the place could use updating. For once, even my husband agrees. I know the other business owners would appreciate any attention you can bring to Silver Ridge."

Optimism filled her. Sydney Ryan never failed to deliver an episode, and her hostess offered an alternative. Becca and Marv wanted Silver Ridge and would get their small, quaint town at Christmas. The network wouldn't get Molly, but Sydney would tackle that issue later. She hugged the woman. "Thanks Cynthia, you're a lifesaver. I would be honored to use the Piñon Gulch Tavern for the episode."

"Only if Jack doesn't agree. He needs you more than we do. I just wish he'd open his eyes and his mind, because you're offering the opportunity of a lifetime. I'll have Larry talk with him." Red crept into the woman's cheeks. "But to be honest, I took advantage of seeing you in the lobby. While you are staying here, I'd like to ask for advice on changes we should make, if you don't mind."

Sydney smiled and winked. "I'd be happy to help. Unlike some people you and I know, I have a knack for that thing."

****

With a fresh cup of coffee, and another angel-shaped sugar cookie, Sydney remained in the lobby to jot down ideas for the Piñon Gulch Tavern. Whether she used the restaurant as an episode, or gave her notes to Cynthia, the concept would be the same. The cozy atmosphere invited her to sit on the lodgepole sofa covered in a soft brown, tan, and cream-colored fabric with images of bears and elk. She kicked off her shoes and stretched her feet toward the fire.

Other guests in the lobby stared and pointed, and she heard a few hushed voices and giggles. Four approached for her autograph. She grimaced. In L.A. she was just another celebrity, but in the small towns, her larger-than-life status always caused a ruckus. Sometimes, she wished she could remain anonymous, but she was grateful for her fans. Without them, she'd have no show.

The fire's heat warmed her, and she twisted a loose section of hair around her pointer finger, watching the orange and gold flames consume the logs. She couldn't think of anything better than sitting by the crackling fire and enjoying the aroma of burning wood and fresh pine, unless she shared the moment with someone.

Sydney shifted. Where had that thought come from? Her career fulfilled her. She needed nothing. Molly's image rose in her mind's eye, then Jack's. Nonsense. Even if she was attracted, which she wasn't, their lives were here, and hers was everywhere but here.

Her phone rang. After a glance at the name, Sydney thought about letting her producer go to voicemail, but she knew Becca would continue calling until she answered. "Becca. How's Tabby doing? How about you?"

"We're both better. Nice diversion. I need an update, Syd."

She sighed and continued to twist her hair. "Nothing yet."

"Still? What have you been doing?"

Staring at the flames again, Sydney ignored the exasperation in Becca's voice. "I tried again today. Right now, I'm enjoying a cup of coffee and cozying up to the fire in the hotel lobby, figuring out another approach. You should make the trip, Becca. You're right. This place is gorgeous."

"Wow. Do I detect longing in your voice? A sense of the always-on-the-go Sydney Ryan, considering staying put longer than a week?"

"Nice try. I'm spending Christmas in the Caymans. Then I'll be back in L.A. before I head to Santa Fe. I thought you might like to see the town firsthand."

"And that, my dear, is why we're running the episode as a Christmas special. No can do. The morning sickness hits every two hours. Lauren will handle the episode, but you can text me pictures. The crew arrives Saturday, so don't take no for an answer."

Across the lobby, Sydney saw Cynthia talking with another woman. When Sydney made eye contact, she smiled and waved at the hotel owner. "You'll get your production, Becca, don't worry. I've got people rooting for me."

"But not the right one."

"I'm on it. I'll let you know when he signs the contract." She disconnected the call.

Sydney Ryan would put this town back on the map. While she could use Cynthia's place as an alternative, she wouldn't give up on Jack or Molly. They needed her, and she needed them. This remodel wasn't about her contract or pleasing her producers. This remodel wasn't just about fixing Joe's Café so Jack could leave a legacy to Molly. This remodel was about something intangible she couldn't quite place.

After settling deeper in the sofa, she stared through the large row of glass windows and viewed the distant snow-covered mountains. The insignificance of her current situation, compared to the permanence of the mountains that struggled against the elements for millions of years, reassured her.

She wouldn't quit trying until she got Jack to sign the paperwork. Sydney Ryan would not be kept down.

****

"Miss Sydney! Over here."

Lost jotting down more ideas for Cynthia and Larry's restaurant, Sydney barely registered a child's voice calling her name. She glanced around the lobby and saw Molly grin and wave as she pulled her father's hand. A frown creased Jack's lips, making her wonder if he ever smiled. "Molly. So good to see you again."

"You, too, Ms. Sydney. I was hoping you'd be here. Look." Molly twirled, displaying her green dress, complimented by red tights and black patent leather shoes. Yesterday's braid hung down her back, but a matching green ribbon hid the hair tie.

"You look beautiful, Molly. What's the occasion?"

"I'm here for a birthday party. We're having afternoon tea in the Mother Lode room," Molly whispered. "I've never been in there before. I think the room is for grown-ups, but Morgan's mom knows the owners."

Behind Molly, Jack swayed, his white-knuckled grip held the green-and-red-striped gift bag.

So, Molly was attending the party Cynthia mentioned earlier. Sydney knew she'd enjoy herself. "Tea is for everyone, but there are certain rules and expectations for young ladies. I bet you won't have any problems though."

The girl puffed out her chest and tapped. "Not me, but I bet Emma Wainwright will, right, Daddy?"

Jack cleared his throat and glanced at his phone.

"We need to leave. The party starts in five minutes."

Molly tugged on his arm. "Can Ms. Sydney redo my braid? I want to look my extra special best. Please, Daddy?"

"I'm sure Ms. Ryan has other things to do." Jack frowned.

He looked none too pleased to be spending any more time in her company. Well, if she had her way, the next couple of weeks would be pure torture. "Nothing that can't wait. Turn around, Molly. This braid will be extra special for an extra special occasion."

"Fine. I'll be right back. Larry wanted to talk." Jack set the birthday present on the coffee table, spun, and strode away.

Sydney almost felt sorry because she knew the topic of their conversation. Cynthia worked fast. Could Larry convince Jack to do the show? She'd take all the help she could get. Next weekend would be here in a flash, and she had several things to accomplish before her crew arrived, like getting Jack to sign the contract.

A few minutes later, Sydney held the compact mirror she kept in her purse to show Molly her handiwork. Instead of the traditional french braid, Sydney inverted it and wove in the ribbon. "You can't see much, but I hope you like it."

"It's beautiful, Ms. Sydney. Thank you." Molly rewarded her with another hug.

"Time to go, Molly." Jack scraped his icy gaze over her, and his lips thinned.

"Yes, Daddy." Oblivious to the tension, Molly grabbed the birthday present, and then reached for Sydney's hand. "Can you help me pick a hat? Morgan says we must wear one. It's a perireckoset."

"Prerequisite." Bad idea. Sydney didn't need to peek at Jack again. "I have things to do, Molly, but when I took a tour earlier, I saw a nice red hat with a green feather that will go great with your outfit."

"Okay. I'll wear that one. Come on, Daddy. I don't want Emma, or anyone else to grab my hat." Molly dragged Jack away.

Sydney settled in her chair and steeled herself for Jack's wrath.

****

A few minutes later, Jack stormed back to the lobby. He'd left Molly in the tearoom and escaped Lila Bennett's clutches again. The woman refused to take no for an answer like the woman sitting by the fireplace. He towered over her. "I'd like a word with you, *Ms. Ryan*."

His emotions overwhelmed him, and he clenched and unclenched his fists. Marin should have braided Molly's hair today, brought her to the party, and had tea with the other mothers and daughters. Marin and Jack should be working together to fix the café's problems, not an outsider who infatuated his daughter. Life was unfair. Anger, resentment, despair, and helplessness warred inside him, fighting for dominance. Larry's discussion was the final straw.

Sydney arched an eyebrow and pasted on a neutral expression. "Yes?"

"Nice try, *Ms. Ryan*, enlisting others to do your dirty work. Larry, of all people. I haven't changed my mind about you exploiting my restaurant, my family, and my staff to your audience. It won't happen. Ever."

She straightened her lips.

Her green eyes hardened, but not before he saw a flash of emotion disappear in their depths as her gaze darted around the room.

"Sit, Mr. Ransom. You're causing a scene. I didn't talk with Larry, Cynthia did."

"I'll stand, thank you." He plowed a hand through his hair two more times before he scratched his neck. He wanted to pace to burn his pent-up energy, but his feet stayed planted to the carpet. More anger coiled in his gut. "Cynthia? You must have talked. How else—"

"I did earlier this afternoon. She introduced herself and gave me a tour of the hotel. We had an interesting conversation."

Jack didn't intimidate her. Why would he? She worked for the infamous Chef Bruno. If he hadn't been so angry, he might have admired her. "And what was that?"

"She figured out why I was here when I mentioned receiving Mary-Katerina Quinn's letter. She also understood the impact my filming here would have on Silver Ridge. In her exact words, Mr. Ransom, *you're not the only business struggling in this town*."

"Be that as it may, *Ms. Ryan,* the answer is still no." Jack turned on his heel and strode away.

Chapter Five

When Sydney entered through the front door of the museum early Monday evening, she stepped back in time.

"Welcome to the Silver Ridge Historical Museum Charity Fundraiser." The elderly docent dressed in faded jeans, a plaid shirt, and red suspenders greeted her.

The man wore an old miner's hat from days gone by, and his voice was gruff from years of smoking. With his bushy beard and grizzled appearance, Sydney envisioned him as a turn of the century miner. She smiled at his friendliness. "Thanks. I'm glad to be here."

"We are, too. If you have questions, please ask. Drinks and appetizers are in the music room down the hall to the right. Would you like a map and guide to the exhibits?" He held out a piece of laminated paper.

"Yes. Thank you."

"Thanks, Donald." Jack stepped beside her and grabbed the sheet.

He cupped his other palm under her elbow, his touch igniting unwanted sensations, but his appearance gave her another opportunity to change his mind. She should be in business mode, not rationalizing this crazy thing that happened when he was close. Her job demanded her full attention, and yet she realized his nearness made her want to forget everything.

"Hi, Jack. Good to see you again. Please sign our guest book before you leave, Ms. Ryan."

The docent's gravelly voice brought her out of her reverie. "Thanks. I will." Another recognition. She got a lot of attention from the growing crowd. Cynthia must have told half the town Sydney created the appetizers. Whatever brought out the people for the museum's annual fundraiser was good. On the small, metal table on her right, Sydney spied the leather-bound book next to the three-foot Christmas tree decorated with white lights, red balls, gold pinecones, and red bows. She also noticed an old, dented milk pail labeled *Donations*. After opening her wallet, she pulled out a twenty-dollar bill and dropped the money inside.

"What brings you here, *Ms. Ryan*?" Jack whispered in her ear.

His warm breath continued to do funny things inside. "Cynthia invited me. Since I helped the staff make the hors d'oeuvres, she thought I should come and learn about the town's history."

"Did she? The refreshments are this way."

"Where's Molly?" Sydney surveyed the foyer of the Victorian.

He tightened his grip. "My neighbor's watching her. I don't bring her out on school nights."

"I don't blame you, though I think she would have enjoyed herself." Sydney glanced around the wide hallway decorated with wreaths, garland, and bows tied to the old-fashioned lights. More garland and lights wrapped around the banister leading to the second floor labeled off-limits to the public. Christmas music drifted in the air, and the odor from the fireplace mingled with the large, pine candle burning on the small, antique table on her left.

"Do you have children?"

"No." From his closed expression, Sydney guessed his question had more than one meaning. Sydney stared at Jack's long, lean fingers holding her elbow—the same warm and gentle hand that made a great cup of coffee and held her as he escorted her to the hotel the other night. She swallowed and refocused on her goal to renovate Joe's Café.

"We'll get a drink, and then I'll give you a tour."

He guided her into a medium-sized room with bookshelves filled with antique books. Tin relief ceiling tiles added more charm, while their footsteps echoed against the original marble floor. A six-foot Christmas tree lit the corner by the fireplace, and off to the side, a teenager played Christmas songs at the baby grand piano. Silver Ridge knew how to decorate for the holiday. Sydney envisioned filming a few shots here to enhance the footage she'd planned to film of the town.

"Hungry?" Jack led her to the rectangular folding tables layered with white and red tablecloths. Silver trays were piled high with warm and cold appetizers. "Which ones are yours?"

"This is one." Sydney grabbed a bacon-wrapped date and plopped it into her mouth. The flavors exploded on her tongue. When she received Cynthia's request for help with the appetizer menu this morning, Sydney suspected the hotel owner knew Jack would be here, which would give her another chance to work on him. She chose another one. Maybe if he tasted her creations, he'd reconsider. "Here."

Jack opened his mouth and allowed Sydney to put

the appetizer inside. He chewed and raised his eyebrows. "Not bad. What else?"

Sydney selected a stuffed mushroom cap. "The secret is to use a mild or medium Italian sausage to spice up things." Her fingers touched his when Jack took the proffered appetizer, and Sydney forced away her hand. She was here to save Joe's Café, nothing more.

"Okay. Two for two. Anything else?"

She pointed to what remained of the baked brie covered in cranberry sauce. "Cynthia said this appetizer would be a hit. I hope I made enough." Sydney sliced off a piece of cheese, spread it on a wheat cracker, and held out the appetizer. This time she was careful not to touch him again. "This tasty morsel is a sampling of what I can do for your menu."

"Nice try. You don't quit, do you?"

Cold matching the temperature outside filled Jack's eyes. Sydney shivered. "No, and it doesn't look like Cynthia and Larry are either." Sydney ate another date. She wasn't hungry, but she needed to occupy her hands, so she didn't reach out to smooth Jack's angst.

Twenty minutes after introductions to the Board members, Sydney and Jack escaped to the former front hall. Sydney sipped her hot chocolate, allowing the rich, creamy goodness to warm her insides. "Wow. Every room is beautiful." As with the others, a decorated Christmas tree sat to the right of the fireplace, and the sparse furniture had been spread out to recreate a Victorian atmosphere. With so many things to take in, Sydney couldn't focus on any specific piece, but the walls grabbed her attention. Groups of pictures crowded the maroon-and-white floral wallpaper. Time had faded the old black-and-white photographs, while more recent colored ones showed the town's progression.

Jack stopped in front of a figure of a burly man in a five-gallon hat holding a gun. "This is the photograph of our infamous third town marshal, Johnny Black, back in 1887. He was imported from Arizona to cull the town's ruthlessness after the first marshal was run out of town after a week. The second, Charles Smith, lasted a month."

"He looks intimidating."

"He brought law and order to Silver Ridge. Without him this place wouldn't be here."

Sydney looked at the next picture of a striking woman dressed in a black, high-collared, full-length dress with a little poof to the sleeves. "Who's this?"

"Jane Hemingway. Another character. If you look closely, she's holding a cigar."

Amusement laced his voice. "A cigar? I didn't know ladies smoked back then."

"She did in the gambling halls. She was the best gambler in town. Although she moved away in her thirties, she's buried in the cemetery surrounding the old Catholic church downtown."

More black-and-white pictures of the mines, the miners, and the mining equipment lined the far wall. On the opposite side, pictures and descriptions of the Grand Hotel and several Victorian mansions stood out against the backdrop of burgundy-colored paint.

Sydney paused by the photo of the train depot. While waiting for the train, the passengers milled under an awning and watched their suitcases piled on the wood planks. The immature trees reminded her of Molly, and the fun she had making snow angels, and the snowball fight a few days ago. A joy filled her similar to the same sensation of the camaraderie she felt with the man near her, then and now.

"Too bad this photo is black-and-white." Sydney touched the smooth glass protecting the old photo to capture in her memory. "I sense the excitement in the air, can't you? The train depot was beautiful in its day."

"It still is…" Jack rubbed the day's growth of beard. "When I was a kid, I wondered where the people went after they arrived in Denver. What adventures awaited? What exciting things would they see?"

"Interesting. When you thought about those things, I imagined where I wanted to travel and what places I wanted to see."

"Where did you want to go?"

"Australia and snorkeling in the Great Barrier Reefs. England and visiting the Tower of London and enjoying traditional fish and chips. France and climbing to the top of the Eiffel Tower and eating fresh-baked croissants. Italy and imagining the echoes of the gladiators in the Coliseum in Rome and eating pizza." Sydney smiled at the thought left unsaid.

"Figures a chef's trip would revolve around food." He drew his brows together. "What's so funny?"

"Nothing." A giggle escaped before she covered her mouth. Her and her crazy idea. Although one day, her dream would become a reality if no one else could see or hear her.

"You can't laugh and not clue me in on the joke. What is it?" Jack folded his arms as he leaned against the wall next to the picture of the depot.

"Fine. I always wanted to go to Austria and pretend I was Maria von Trapp." She laughed again, imagining herself twirling with open arms in the middle of the Alps.

He gave her a crooked grin before his laughter joined hers. Tapping his fingers against his biceps, Jack stared. "From *The Sound of Music*? Somehow, I can imagine you there. That's one of Molly's favorite movies."

"Mine, too. I've loved it since I was a kid, but I have a problem with my idea." Sydney rolled her eyes. "I can't sing. I sound like a frog."

"Why do I doubt you?"

"Don't. I was encouraged *not* to join the choir in high school."

"If it makes you feel better, I can't sing either, but that doesn't stop me. Ask anyone at the annual Christmas Caroling on the Square festival weekend."

At the thought of Jack singing, she bit back a grin. He didn't look the type to join in the fun. "That's the event Molly told me about the other day, isn't it?"

Jack nodded. "Have you seen any of those places?"

Sydney took the hint he didn't want to talk about Silver Ridge and followed his lead. "Australia, yes, and to the Caribbean, and New Zealand, but not Europe yet. How about you?"

"I've never traveled out of Colorado. Marin and I always wanted to go to Hawaii."

Sadness crossed his handsome features, and Sydney knew Jack thought about his late wife. His continued love still shone through even years after her death. Would Sydney ever experience that kind of devoted love? Would she ever feel love at all? She stiffened, wondering where that errant thought had sprung from. Her current life suited her. What was it about this town that made her question a few of her life decisions?

"I'll take Molly someday."

Jack's words brought her back to the present. "I believe you will." She left her other thoughts unspoken as she stared at the photo again. The depot needed tender loving care, and an owner and his daughter needed love and care, too. Sydney could help. "The building hasn't changed much."

He ran a finger along the rough wood surface. "Aside from the awning and the trees, you're right. My grandparents were adamant about maintaining the structure's integrity and keeping things the same."

A color photograph would have suited her better, but she assumed from Jack's words, what she saw was close to the original design. "Which is why you're opposed to adding anything or becoming part of the twenty-first century."

With a sigh, he straightened the photograph.

A faraway expression crossed the features she'd grown accustomed to.

"Do you have a family heritage, Ms. Ryan?"

"No, so, I apologize if I don't understand the concept. I have no close family either."

"None?" Jack squeezed her elbow and angled her to face him.

She fell into the inky pools of water in his eyes. "I was an only child. I have a few second cousins in the Chicago suburbs and an aunt, an uncle, and a cousin in Florida, but I haven't seen them since my mother's funeral. Outside of the obligatory Christmas card and 'come visit when you're in the area,' I've never heard from them."

"I was an only child, too. Molly has a few cousins on her mother's side outside of Denver. I try and take her to see them once or twice a year."

His sad expression told her the visits weren't as often as he'd like, but he couldn't take away the time from his business, and he didn't have the money to spend.

"My parents died in a car accident the winter after I graduated from high school."

More sadness at another loss in his life consumed her. She and Jack had more in common than she'd first thought. "I'm sorry for your tragic loss."

Jack nodded. "I had Uncle Ray to help me. He took over the restaurant until Marin and I could run the place on our own."

A fond smile curved his lips. Sydney grabbed his hand and squeezed. Why did this man affect her? "You're lucky to have him." Sydney only had her friends. If she had godparents, she never knew of them. "Is he related to your mother or father?"

"I couldn't have survived. Uncle Ray is my godfather. He and my father were best friends. My dad stayed in town while Uncle Ray explored the world in the Navy. After he retired, he came home for a few months and never left."

Alone in the room, the sound of their breathing filled the space. Christmas music filtered in, and pine drifted under her nose. She released his hand and stepped back, breaking the moment. She refocused on the old photo of the depot. "Do you suppose this is the only photo the museum has? I'd like to see an interior shot to get ideas."

"I don't know." Jack shook his head. "It doesn't

matter, does it? No matter how hard you try, you're not using my restaurant as an episode for your show."

Sydney smiled. *That's what you think.*

****

"Good morning, Mrs. Collins. I'm glad you're feeling better." Jack stomped the snow from his shoes and shrugged off his jacket Tuesday morning. He hung it on the coat stand by the front door, the warmth from the fire chasing away the outdoor chill. The aroma of fresh-brewed coffee filled his senses as it had since his childhood. He should be refreshed after a day off, but he wasn't. Far from it.

"Good morning, Mr. Ransom. Much better, but still not one hundred percent. Thanks."

She gave him a speculative glance. Her formal greeting drove him crazy. He still couldn't figure out if Sunday was a coincidence or a conspiracy, but his server did look pale. "That's good news."

"Looks like another cold one. These winters are starting to bother me, and it's only the beginning of December. That might be why I got sick so early in the season." The stout woman placed her hands on her hips and shook her head. "Lordy, my granddaughter keeps telling me to move to Scottsdale. If the weather stays unseasonably cold, I might just leave."

Reliable, friendly, and trustworthy until now, Mrs. Collins was his only full-time server and had worked at Joe's Café for years. Jack couldn't believe his uncle and Mrs. Collins had done behind his back and, through Molly, caught Sydney Ryan's attention. Should convince Mrs. Collins to make good on her threat to move? "The snow's early this year. That's good for the ski resorts and for us. How was business this morning?"

He rubbed his hands together to generate more warmth.

"Okay. The weather is keeping everyone inside."

"Or the after-holiday lull. Happens every year." Jack walked behind the counter and poured himself a cup of coffee. Then he dumped in a packet of sweetener and stirred before taking a sip of the hot brew. He would never tire of the taste. If he didn't lose the restaurant. Heaviness filled his heart.

He glanced around the room. A few customers in various stages of eating filled three of the tables, and two needed to be cleared. Okay, so Mrs. Collins had slowed over the past few years, but she was an indispensable and valued employee. Molly and the customers loved her. He suspected his uncle liked her, too, and that thought brought a smile to his lips. Both Mr. Collins and Aunt Kathryn died almost twelve years ago. Jack would like his two favorite employees to find companionship in each other's arms. "Where's Uncle Ray?"

Mrs. Collins wedged a bus tub on her hip and slapped a wet towel over the edge. She smoothed a non-existent piece of dyed, dark brown hair. "In the kitchen. Frank and Max both called in sick today. Whatever they have is just awful."

"Great." Jack scraped a hand through his hair. Not what he needed right now. Tuesday was slow, but Wednesday mornings were decent because he had two separate groups between six and ten people that came in one after the other. He hoped his employees got better soon.

"Yes. Poor things. They both sounded terrible. Same nasty thing I had Sunday. How did you manage?"

The sound of chairs scraping on the floor caught

his attention.

"Bye, Mr. and Mrs. Wellington. Come back soon." Mrs. Collins waved to the departing couple.

"We managed." Jack thought of Sydney Ryan again. Having her at Joe's Café felt natural. Without her help, he wouldn't have kept up on Sunday, and that could hurt what remained of the restaurant's reputation, but that was where he drew the line. He didn't need her to repaint the interior or move the tables and chairs.

"Hi, Jack." Uncle Ray carried a rack of coffee mugs and water glasses to the counter. The squeaky door to the kitchen closed behind him as he unloaded them, the blue veins a contrast against his white, wrinkled skin. "Heard we had an important person fill in for Mrs. Collins Sunday."

"About that…" Jack went to replace the sugar in the ceramic ramekins, but his fingers tightened around the white packets, crushing them. Uncle Ray's and Mrs. Collins' meddling put his café on the reality TV star's radar. Molly couldn't have come up with the idea alone.

"Goodbye, folks, stop in again." Uncle Ray spoke to another couple vacating the window table.

"Who was here on Sunday? What did I miss?" Mrs. Collins huffed as she set the half-full bus tub on the counter. "Sheesh, you call in sick, and they're ready to put you out to pasture."

Uncle Ray grabbed Mrs. Collins' hand and kissed the back. He had a twinkle in his eyes, and his smile created more wrinkles around his faded lips. "Now, now, Suzette. I'll make certain no one will take your place here."

Crimson stained the older woman's cheeks. Jack raised his eyebrows. His uncle had called her by her first name. Interesting. He'd been so preoccupied; he hadn't seen the budding romance between them. "Don't worry, Mrs. Collins. Your job's safe."

Mrs. Collins fanned herself. "Well, that's a relief. I'm no spring chicken, you know. It would be hard to find another job at my age."

Uncle Ray gave her a crooked smile and pulled the bus tub from the counter. "I like seasoned chicken. Sydney Ryan can't hold a candle to you."

"Sydney Ryan was *here*? The *Sydney Ryan* from *Ryan to the Rescue*? In Joe's Café?" Mrs. Collins sputtered and raised a hand to her heart.

"Yes." As if she didn't know. News traveled fast in Silver Ridge. Jack caught the subtle, but pleased, look passing between his two employees. Bingo. They *were* the masterminds behind Molly's letter. He wanted to be angry when his daughter mentioned their names, but he couldn't. If he didn't love his uncle and respect his employee, he'd still be upset at the dissention. They only had his best interests at heart.

The bell over the front door jingled. Jack turned to greet the guests, but his words strangled in his throat. "Good morning, Ms. Ryan." The woman was relentless.

****

"Good morning, Mr. Ransom." Sydney strode to the counter and set her bag and the folder containing some ideas and the contract on the worn surface. He looked anything but happy saying those words, and the tight smile matched the darkness in his eyes. The aroma of fresh ground coffee filled her senses, and her mouth watered. "A cup of coffee, please."

She unbuttoned her coat. Once she fixed the place, Joe's Café would be warm and cozy, and make people linger after their meals. She needed Jack's permission to start.

"Did you want to sit at a table? I'll bring it over."

"I'll stay here." She placed her coat over the back of the stool and sat. Sydney watched Jack turn away, giving her a full view of his backside. Dark, wavy hair brushed the collar of his maroon and black flannel shirt. His broad shoulders stooped under the weight of keeping this place open. His rolled sleeves revealed muscular arms sprinkled with hair as he poured her coffee. Sydney swallowed when she caught the fresh scent of his masculine cologne. Her heart skipped a beat, and she found it difficult to catch her breath. Not good. The man affected her equilibrium.

A few moments later, Jack set her cup on the counter and slid it toward her, avoiding contact.

"Is Molly at school?"

"Yes."

"Good." Another uncomfortable silence lingered. She traced her fingertips along the edge of a stain. She'd have her crew refinish the wood instead of covering the surface with a place mat. "I thought I'd show you a few potential ideas."

Jack wiped the counter with a white cloth.

The familiar scent of bleach filled her nose. Some things never changed.

He slapped down the towel and folded his arms, his eyes narrowing. The tic in his cheek became more prominent. As he looked at the space behind her head, a scowl twisted his lips.

His eyes darkened to cobalt, and she felt a shift between them.

"What don't you understand, Ms. Ryan? The

answer is still no. Too much of my family's history is in here to let you wipe it all away and make it sterile like you've done on your episodes."

"Then why do you watch my show?" Sydney pulled the paper outlining her proposal for Joe's Café from the folder. She'd only been in the restaurant seven hours Sunday, but she'd had a lot of time to think the last couple of days. She placed the sheet in front of him. "Here's what I propose."

"Let me look." He pulled the paper toward him and wedged his hands against his forehead.

Silence filled the space until Sydney heard him chuckle under his breath as he shook his head.

"Not happening. No way. What? Are you crazy? Vegetarian options?" He pushed the paper back across the counter. "Tofu is not food."

"Not crazy. Just a realist. Tofu has its place in American and Asian cuisine." Sydney stared at the tic in Jack's cheek.

His brows furrowed, and a straight line creased his lips. "What you're proposing is ridiculous."

Sydney tensed and fisted her palms. "It is not, Jack. You've watched my show. You know what I'm all about. What I do." She squared her shoulders and inhaled. "Nothing written on that list is ridiculous or unnecessary. I will make Joes Café successful again."

"I just need a little help. Not what you've outlined there." He waved at her paperwork.

She couldn't find a way to soften her words. This place meant a lot to Jack and Molly, by the letter she received from his daughter, but in its present state, she figured the café would close before the end of summer. "You need me, Jack. You know you do."

"What's wrong with the menu?" Jack pounded a fist on the counter, rattling her coffee cup and spoon. "Why can't we slop on paint and refinish the tables and chairs?"

Sydney wanted to understand his frustration. She'd worked with difficult owners before, but they'd always come around to see her vision. Then again, Jack hadn't written her, Molly had, which was a big difference. Still, she offered simple solutions. "Look at this place and tell me what you see."

"I see the labor of love of my parents and grandparents."

She followed his gaze to the faded, outdated posters of Germany on the wall behind the counter. The old castle nestled in the mountains, the medieval town with cobblestone streets, and the vineyard on the slopes of the Rhine River had to go. Even the painted sign Molly pointed out on Sunday had chipped paint and needed to be refinished.

"I'm sorry, Jack, but that's part of the problem." Sydney lowered her voice and put a hand on his arm. Mistake. Energy singed her insides. She pulled away her hand, but not before the damage was done. "You're so stuck in the past, you can't see the present or the future. If there is a future. Right now, I'm not sure the café has one."

"This place has been in my family for fifty years, and I'll figure out how to keep it open, so Molly has an inheritance."

This time Sydney heard Jack's hesitation as he gripped the counter. "I don't see it that way, Jack." Sydney grabbed her list and set it on top of the contract. She clenched and unclenched her fists and stared at the man refusing her help. The ideas she proposed were solid, but the past blinded his ability to see the bleak future.

Unless he allowed her to make over his restaurant, or he did something drastic, this place would close. What else could she do to change his mind? While Cynthia offered her a solution, it wouldn't be enough for her network, and she could kiss her new contract goodbye.

Chapter Six

At three minutes to four Wednesday morning, Sydney shivered inside her jacket and waited for Uncle Ray to arrive and unlock the door. She should have stayed in her rental car. Icy wind whipped around the back of the building and slipped under her collar. Brutal. The temperate climate of L.A. was a distant memory. Still, the frigid air invigorated her, and so did the idea of fixing this place. If Jack agreed, this makeover would be her all-time favorite.

Headlights slashed through the darkness as a vehicle drove into the rear lot. A second one followed close behind. Sydney waved at the driver pulling into the closest spot, and the woman waved back. An older model white SUV pulled in next to the first vehicle, and when the lights dimmed, she recognized Uncle Ray. Shoving her hands in her pockets, she waited.

Uncle Ray hustled to open the woman's car door and helped her from her seat. When he held her arm as he walked her to the back door, Sydney smiled at the sweet gesture. The old man thought enough of the older woman to make sure she didn't slip on the ice. Chivalry at its finest. Saturday night's escort to the hotel burned in her brain, and she swore she felt Jack's touch on her arm again. "Good morning, Mr. Donaldson."

"Call me Ray. Good morning to you, too, Sydney." Uncle Ray motioned to the other woman. "This is

Suzette Collins."

The older woman smoothed her hair before offering a hand. "Pleased to meet you, Sydney. I can't believe we have a real, live celebrity in our tiny town."

"Pleased to meet you, too, Mrs. Collins. Like I told your cousin, Cynthia, there's no need to treat me any different. I'm human." Sydney smiled at the flustered woman with the warm and welcoming expression and shook her hand.

"Cynthia said you were nice, and I see she was right. Please call me Suzette, dear. Only Molly and Jack call me Mrs. Collins. It drives him crazy, right, Ray?" Suzette patted his arm.

She gave him an adoring look that seemed to signal a private joke. Sydney fought a smile.

"Just remember to call me Mrs. Collins when he's in earshot." Mrs. Collins winked.

"Got it." Sydney widened her grin and winked back. Working with these two would be a piece of cake. Jack's dour expression rose in her mind's eye. He would be a challenge in more than ways of the heart. "Are you sure your idea will work? My crew arrives in three days."

"It has to. He's simply a big idiot and needs more convincing. We're on your side, along with a lot of other people in town. We've been after Jack to fix this place for years, but he's as stubborn as a mule. He says he won't because of the family heritage. I think he's afraid." Uncle Ray unlocked the door and ushered her inside. "Both Max and Frank will call in sick again today, so you'll have full charge of the kitchen until Jack gets here at nine. I'll help you if it gets busy, but otherwise I'll be the dishwasher and busboy."

"Are they sick?" Concern laced Sydney's voice.

Ray and Suzette laughed.

"Sick of working in a tired, outdated kitchen and restaurant." Suzette waved a hand.

"A little bribery helped, too." Uncle Ray flipped the light switch before he disabled the alarm on the pad next to the door. "The code's one-four-nine-two. You'll need it if no one is here when you leave."

Sydney nodded. "Once Jack agrees, I won't need access until the actual production days."

The old man shrugged out of his coat and hung it on the antique coat rack in the corner. Then he helped Suzette from hers before reaching for Sydney's.

"Thanks." She hoped the rickety contraption didn't fall apart under the weight. Glancing around the office transported her back in time. Three tall windows flanked by dark-brown-trimmed crown molding ran almost the entire length of the left wall. More crown molding bordered the doorway to the restaurant, while a chair rail separated the faded yellow paint on the walls from the dark wood paneling on the bottom. An old, scarred, wooden desk littered with magazines and piles of paper sat under the windows, while a larger desk with shelves and nooks dominated the opposite wall. Only a computer and touchtone telephone signaled the twenty-first century. "Who came up with that code?"

"Molly." Suzette tucked her purse in a desk drawer. "Such a sweet child. It's such a shame—put your pocketbook in here, dear." Suzette signaled to drop her tiny bag inside. "Jack lets her disable the alarm on the weekends. He wanted her to pick numbers she could remember without using birthdate dates."

"One-four-nine-two." Sydney repeated the set of

numbers. It always helped her memory to say things out loud. "Fourteen-ninety-two." An old childhood rhyme echoed in her brain. "In fourteen hundred ninety-two Columbus sailed the ocean blue…Columbus. I won't forget it now. How original."

"That's our Molly." Uncle Ray smiled.

Suzette wedged her hands against her ample hips. "I wish that boy would remarry. Molly should have another mother."

"Suzette." Uncle Ray frowned, shaking his head.

Disgusted, the woman flailed her arms. "Not talking about it doesn't mean it doesn't exist. Marin died three years ago. Jack needs to move on."

Ray crossed his arms. "Enough. Jack will decide when he's ready."

"When will that be?" Suzette huffed.

Sydney's attention flipped between the two as if she watched a table tennis match. Ray and Suzette argued like the old married couples she saw on TV. Somehow, she sensed they'd had this discussion before, but in private, reminding her she was an outsider.

"We took twelve years, and even then, some days still aren't that easy." Uncle Ray lowered his voice and reached out to stroke Suzette's arm.

The conversation stopped, but she couldn't help but think about their words. Her heart went out to Jack and Molly for their loss. She hoped someday soon Jack could move on and find another woman to love and give his daughter a stepmother.

"Everything put away? This way." Ray ushered her toward the kitchen.

Sydney grabbed a lungful of air. Despite her lack of morning coffee, energy coursed through her. "Did you get everything on my list?"

"And then some. Everything's in the walk-in or on the counter. Let me know how I can help." Ray held the kitchen door.

"Me, too." Suzette added. "Let me make the coffee first, though. I'm not used to getting here this early."

"Don't worry, Suzette. Now that I have a key and the code, I'll come and go as I please." Sydney glanced around the kitchen, which hadn't gotten any bigger since Sunday. Six of Jack's kitchens could fit inside the last kitchen she'd renovated. There she'd joked about needing rollerblades, where here she had everything at her fingertips. She'd like to add more space, but her show helped the owner work with what he or she already had, not build additions. She'd create more room with storage, modernizing the equipment, and reorganizing the shelves and counters.

A few hours later, Sydney wiped her forehead. Jack had yet to arrive, so Uncle Ray helped her behind the line. "Ray, if Joe's Café was your restaurant, what changes would you make?" Sydney always talked to the staff to get their perspective on how things should operate. If she had their permission, she'd also interview them for her show.

"Aside from renovating the entire kitchen and seating area, I'd change the menu."

"In what way?" Even though Sydney had put a few of her ideas in process today, she wanted to hear what the staff had to say.

"I dunno, but there's got to be more to breakfast than bacon and eggs." Uncle Ray dumped the hash browns next to the under-cooked bacon and set the plate on the counter. "He's stuck in a rut. Same outdated food and interior. If I didn't love the boy so much—"

"I agree. Please change the menu. Add more variety. Make it healthier. Do more of what you've done today." Suzette chimed as she clipped a piece of paper to the clip order wheel mounted under the shelf above the prep counter. "Order in. I have friends that won't come in here because everything is fried or loaded with calories. Even the backward grocery store is coming to terms with the new clientele and offering an organic section in their produce department. Jack is way behind the times."

"He's stuck in the seventies." Ray nodded.

"We all agree his décor is, too." Sydney flipped the pancakes. Finding her roots and being behind the line again felt good, and not just for the show. Normally she wouldn't intrude into the inner workings of the restaurant outside of creating new items or updating existing ones, but she couldn't resist Ray and Suzette's plan. If this idea didn't work, nothing would.

****

At five minutes after ten, Jack walked through the office door, removed his jacket, and threw it over the back of his chair. Frustration eroded his composure. A dead battery delayed his arrival, and he didn't know what to expect when he walked into the dining area.

He clapped his hands together to get the blood flowing and shouldered the door. Aside from his routine party of seven today, only six other patrons lingered at the tables. Frustration bit the edges of his sanity as he shoved his fingers through his hair. He needed to figure out how to create more business, not swallow his pride and allow a TV celebrity to expose his restaurant to the world. "Good morning, Uncle Ray. How'd the morning go?" Jack strode to the counter where the old man wiped the service area.

"Frank and Max are out again, but everything's under control. Everything okay with your truck?"

"Needed a battery, but water pump's bad." He'd bought the truck a few months before Molly's birth, and with over one hundred and twenty thousand miles, the vehicle showed its age.

"That'll set you back a couple hundred bucks."

His uncle busied himself doing Mrs. Collins' job of placing stir sticks in the white ceramic container, then refilling the sugar and sweetener packets. Why? Nothing went according to plan since Sydney Ryan appeared in Silver Ridge. Tired, Jack passed a hand across his face.

"I know." Jack opened the cash register and thumbed through the bills to see if he needed to get cash from the safe. The till wasn't as full as it should be. After he closed the drawer, a sinking feeling erupted in his stomach. He shook his head. His uncle wouldn't. "So, Uncle Ray, if you're out here, and Frank and Max are sick, who's in the kitchen?"

His uncle simply smiled, aggravating him further. He strode from the register and burst through the kitchen door.

"Good morning, Mr. Ransom. Happy Wednesday." Sydney greeted him.

Her smile and fresh energy twisted his insides into a tangled mess. The woman haunting his dreams worked behind the line. He captured her gaze, leaving him out of breath like he'd run a marathon through green goo. Suddenly, he felt like that gawky teenager again.

"Morning, Ms. Ryan." Jack growled, rubbing his eyes, too tired to get angry that everyone conspired against him. He needed an IV filled with coffee to jump start his brain so he could think. Why did this woman wreak havoc on him in his daytime hours, and now his nighttime ones? Sleep had evaded him. She'd been on his mind all night, and each time he closed his eyelids, he saw her pink-tinted lips and generous smile. Jack shuddered at an image of him hugging her when he drifted off. He didn't need this complication. "Why are you here?

"I stopped in to talk to you, not realizing you came in late. Frank and Max are still sick, and Uncle Ray couldn't handle the kitchen alone, so I volunteered again."

He didn't buy Sydney's innocence as she flipped the eggs with one hand and the potatoes with the other.

"I come in after I drop off Molly at school. Volunteer? You just happened to have your chef jacket with you? How convenient." Another piece of paper and a pen sat on the back counter. What now? The woman was relentless. He scraped a hand through his hair as frustration warred with anger.

"Any thoughts about what I said yesterday?" Sydney slid the eggs on a plate.

"No." She'd brought up valid points and things he chose not to address for fear of being disloyal to his family and heritage, but at what cost? Jack owned a dying restaurant stuck in the seventies with a clientele who matched the outdated interior. He wanted to care but hadn't since Marin died. As he looked around the kitchen, he took in the well-used equipment and inefficient workspace. More frustration weighed on his shoulders. The restaurant was the only connection he had to his parents, grandparents, and Marin.

He shrugged away his thoughts. Other things consumed him. "What do you have here?" While tying on his apron, Jack stepped behind the line to help Sydney with the three tickets hanging on the rack. Even though she had the situation handled, he wanted to make certain the food met his standards, not hers. Knowing her, she'd arrange it on the plate like a piece of art.

"Nothing I can't handle." Sydney flipped the pancakes on the grill.

"A yogurt bowl?" Jack widened his eyes as he yanked the order slip from the line. "We don't have yogurt here."

"You do as a special this morning. I've tried extra menu items to gauge customer reactions. The rest of the order is ready." She plated the two pieces of thick french toast. "Can you get the yogurt from the walk-in?"

"Where's the regular bread? What are onions and peppers doing in the potatoes?" He opened his mouth. "What are you doing to my restaurant? Where did you get the ingredients?" Jack growled, resisting the urge to crumple the piece of paper and throw it across the kitchen. Was he living in a nightmare? He pinched himself to see if he was awake. *Ouch*.

"The grocery store. I have fresh cut fruit that goes with the yogurt. Can you bring that container as well?" Sydney ran a clean rag along the edges of the plates. After placing a sliced strawberry and a twisted orange slice next to the sausage links, she put the two plates on the serving shelf and rang the bell.

"Fruit? That's a waste of time and money. Nobody eats garnish."

"The presentation is more appealing. I thought you watched my show."

Jack mangled the rag he'd removed from the counter and seethed under his breath so his other staff and the customers couldn't hear. "I do, while reading the news. I didn't give you permission to do anything here."

Sydney just smiled. "I'm enhancing what you already have, and everything's been well received. I told Mrs. Collins to offer the traditional items or my version, and so far, only one person has ordered it the old way. People are eating the garnish. The yogurt and fruit, please?"

He stomped to the walk-in and manhandled the door. What else would he find when he did inventory? Five loaves of the thick bread, more fruits and vegetables, two bags of heirloom potatoes, and three family packs of short ribs. He sank against the rack behind him, the chill permeating him to the core. What was Sydney plotting? And what…

The green-and-white packet on the shelf mocked him. Extricating the tofu between finger and thumb, he stared. She didn't. She did. Jack marched back to the grill and held up the package. "What is tofu doing here?"

"I bought it for you."

A wicked grin brightened her face. "That stuff will go nowhere near my or my customer's mouths. Understood?"

"The yogurt, please? You're affecting my timing."

Without a pause, Sydney continued plating the orders.

Jack stomped back to the refrigerator and threw the tofu on the shelf instead of the garbage. His practical side wouldn't let him waste the subhuman food. After grabbing the fruit and the tub of yogurt, he forced himself behind the line. At this rate, he would never allow her to renovate his restaurant. He lifted the lid off the plastic container next to the unwanted tray of strawberries and orange slices. "What's in here?"

"Homemade granola to go with the yogurt. Can you dish some into a bowl, please?"

He felt like a stick caught in a raging river. He fought the current carrying him downstream but lost the battle. In a matter of days, Sydney Ryan had entered his restaurant and tilted everything off axis.

"Here." Sydney handed him a bowl.

Jack scooped the granola, dumped it in, and pushed it toward her. "What time did you come in this morning?"

"Does it matter?" Sydney plated the last of the order and wedged the ticket under the plate of toast as Mrs. Collins bustled into the kitchen.

"The Newtons are raving about your french toast, and their daughter is glad you have a yogurt special. She wants the recipe for the granola." She put the order slip into her pocket and pulled the plates from the window. "I told them it would be a new item, and they had to keep coming back. They also want to know what else you have up your sleeve."

"Tell them to keep coming back." Sydney's laughter spilled out as she wiped the counter.

More uneasiness saturated the surrounding space. Her menu changes were a hit with both the customers and his staff. Word had gotten out Sydney Ryan considered using his place for an episode, and people crawled out of the woodwork to grab the chance to see the celebrity. Jack noticed a spring in Mrs. Collins' step as she walked away. Sydney brought back life into the restaurant before he'd even agreed to the work. If he did. If only he could get as excited as he watched the graceful way she used the spatula to wipe the excess food from the grill. "Is that why I found short ribs in the walk-in?"

"Yep."

"What other specials should I know about?"

"Apple pancakes and short rib hash. I've sold five of each already today."

"Ms. Ryan." Jack elongated her name and clenched his fists. "I did not give you permission to do anything. I don't want you back here. You're a liability nightmare. I don't care what my uncle and Mrs. Collins are doing, or the Langley's across the street. This is my restaurant. The answer is still no."

****

Between the breakfast and lunch crowd, Sydney scrubbed the griddle with the pumice stone. The ache in her arms increased with each stroke, but the release of her suppressed anger felt good. Ray and Suzette's plan had not worked. She continued the circular motion, careful not to let her hands slip and bang against the hot surface. Her irritation didn't warrant another battle scar. Why didn't Jack recognize her show would save his restaurant? Why did he refuse her help? The changes wouldn't cost him a dime outside of purchasing the additional items she'd put on the menu. "Of all the obstinate, obtuse, stubborn—"

"You missed pig-headed."

Sydney dropped the stone on the griddle and jumped backward. She hadn't seen or heard Jack enter the kitchen, much less pick up a rag and wipe the counter. Keeping a focus on his powerful grip was better than staring at the tightlipped man. His darkened expression tried to pierce her thick skin, but it wouldn't work. She'd stood firm against more intimidating figures.

"I'm getting there." She wiped her forehead with her sleeve before she continued to clean the griddle. "Did you need something, Mr. Ransom?" A stagnant pause permeated the air. The tinny, seventies, classic rock song from the radio on the shelf behind the line, and the scraping of the stone against steel broke the ragged sound of their breathing.

"No."

Her crew arrived in three days, and for the first time in her career, she had no restaurant to film. At least she had a Plan B, even though she didn't want to give up on Joe's Café. Time and Jack were not her friends right now, and her frustration mounted. "You're behind the times, Jack Ransom, with your drinks and your menus. If you don't do it for yourself, do the renovation for Molly. She's only eight, but she seems to be the only one in the Ransom family who understands and appreciates what I'm offering."

"Leave my daughter out of this discussion. I don't want to make changes here, Ms. Ryan. When will you understand?"

She yanked the towel from her apron, wiped her hands, and threw it on the counter. "I'll never understand why you refuse to do what's in the café's best interests. You could have a successful place here, with a line out the door during the season, if you let me work my magic. Take off your blinders, Mr. Ransom. This place has potential to be a gold mine. Quit being so obtuse, stubborn, and pig-headed, and—"

****

"Don't forget obstinate." Jack growled. His pulse quickened, and he didn't appreciate his reaction to Sydney when her eyes lit with anger. If he thought her beautiful before, she was more so now. She was a danger to his equilibrium, and his way of life. Her presence challenged his faithfulness to the memories of Marin, because all he wanted to do was kiss the blonde and absorb her passion for his restaurant.

He used to have that emotion, but it died along with his wife. "Go away, Ms. Ryan. When will you understand I don't want you, or your ideas, here?" As if an idea clicked in her brain, her expression softened, and pity fluttered across her face.

She reached for her cell phone in her jacket pocket. "Okay, Mr. Ransom, I won't ask you again."

She was giving up? He actually enjoyed sparring with her. "What are you doing?"

"I'm calling my producer."

He watched her punch in a number. Unease and distrust resided in his stomach. "Why?"

"Like you, I have a job to do, Mr. Ransom. My producer wants an episode filmed in Silver Ridge, and I'll give her one. I'm making her aware Joe's Café won't work, but I've found an alternate." She continued to stare. "Hi, Becca."

"What other place?" Jack should have guessed she had something up her sleeve. He crossed his arms, knowing he didn't intimidate her, but he couldn't help himself. She bothered him, and despite her expertise and the fact he could use some help, he didn't want her here. Still, as she mentioned, she had a job to do and a living to make. Although right now, he suspected her ability to earn was a lot higher.

"Hang on." She covered the phone again. "The Piñon Gulch Tavern."

"The Piñon Gulch Tavern in the Grand Hotel?" Incredulous, Jack paced the small confines of the kitchen. He didn't understand why the news upset him. He should be happy Sydney Ryan was moving to another location.

"Yes. Cynthia and Larry suspected you wouldn't agree and offered me their place. The Piñon Gulch Tavern meets all the requirements and will satisfy my producer."

"Unbelievable. Their restaurant is in much better shape."

She narrowed her gaze. "True, but they're willing to work with me." Sydney uncovered the phone and turned slightly. "Hey, Becca. I'll call you later."

He saw her ruthless, take-no-prisoner attitude that allowed her to get her way on her show. Something inside him shifted as he scraped a hand through his hair. He glanced to the kitchen door to make sure his uncle or Mrs. Collins were nowhere in sight. "My restaurant's not good enough for your show?" His voice sliced through the air.

"Not anymore. Your pride and ego got in the way." Sydney dropped her phone back in her pocket.

"My pride and ego are not the problem here." Jack trapped her behind the line.

She shrugged and stepped back. "Then what is? You're afraid Sydney Ryan will make a success of Joe's Café?"

"I'm not afraid." Sweat formed on his brow, and his heart rate increased. *Or was he?*

"That's not what I see." Her eyebrows rose, and she pursed her lips. "Now if you'll excuse me, I have work to do across the street."

Her nonchalant attitude irritated him further. His place needed help. Sydney knew her stuff, but to have her here every day when he saw her passion and wanted to touch it for himself? Or seeing Molly grow more attached to the woman she'd idolized on television? Was that the reason he was against her help? At what cost? The way his business decreased, he'd have nothing left to leave Molly, and the loss of her legacy would be his fault.

Anger, bitterness, and resignation warred inside. "Fine. You win. Bring in your ideas, your camera crews, and your staff. Do what you want here." He paced back and forth, his voice clipped. "Molly is off limits. No interviews or filming, or I will cancel the entire renovation thing."

"I understand. You won't regret it. Thank you." A smile lit her face, and Sydney gave him a quick hug.

He kept his hands to his sides so he didn't reach out and draw her tempting warmth closer.

What had he just done?

Chapter Seven

Jack had fallen for Sydney's charms and agreed to let her into his life for the next week or two, hours at a time. She'd duped him and manipulated him into agreeing to the makeover when she mentioned Larry and Cynthia and the Piñon Gulch Tavern.

He regretted his decision.

Seconds later, he grabbed her folder and strode from the kitchen. Once in his favorite counter seat, he strangled the stained, white coffee cup as he stared at the dark liquid, searching for an answer. For the first time in his life, he had none. He had so much to do today, but his body refused to obey his mind.

Under other circumstances, he'd talk to Uncle Ray, but his uncle had cast his lot with Sydney Ryan. So had the Langleys, and if what the owners of the Grand Hotel said yesterday, so did several business owners in Silver Ridge. This restaurant meant the world to Jack, and to Molly.

Was letting Sydney Ryan have her way the right thing to do? He'd given a verbal agreement but hadn't signed the contract. Jack studied the papers on the folder. Marin visited him in a dream last night and told him he'd be a fool if he didn't accept Sydney's help. Everything she outlined made sense for Joe's Café, so what was his problem?

Sydney Ryan. She meant trouble to his emotions,

and heart, if he let her close. Maybe that was the reason he'd been so adamant about not having her use his café on *Ryan to the Rescue*.

"What's that?" Uncle Ray shuffled behind the counter.

"Paperwork."

"Looks like a proposal."

He didn't buy the innocent look while his uncle appeared to be adjusting his hearing aid. Moments later, Jack swore he saw him wink at Mrs. Collins as she walked by to retrieve the coffee pot. "Uncle Ray…" Jack picked out a packet of sugar from the white ceramic ramekin and crushed it in his fist. Uncle Ray's and Mrs. Collins' meddling forced him to let the TV star into his life and restaurant, for a week or more, depending on how long production took.

Sydney joined him once Uncle Ray went into the kitchen to prep for the small lunch crowd.

"Any questions, Mr. Ransom?" Sydney sat on the next stool.

Her voice enveloped him like a warm blanket. "Since it appears we'll be working together for the next two weeks, call me Jack."

"Okay, Jack. Please call me Sydney."

Jack liked the way his name rolled off her tongue, like the babbling brook trickling over stones at the park outside of town in the spring. But he shouldn't. Sydney Ryan was trouble with a capital T. His daughter had fallen hard for the celebrity who entered their house every week via television. If he wasn't careful, he might do the same. His heart couldn't take another loss. How fast could she film the show? Frowning, he motioned to the table they'd sat at Sunday and growled,

"Did you want to sit over there?"

****

"No. The counter is fine. Did you change your mind?" Guilt nipped at Sydney's conscience when she thought about how she'd manipulated him into letting her use his restaurant. But if he wanted a legacy for Molly, he had no choice.

"You can film your production here. Even I recognize I need help, but I will keep full control of the makeover and the food. I must approve everything. Is that stipulation understood, Sydney?"

"Clear as day, Jack." She would honor his requests as long as he agreed with her plans. She had standards to uphold, viewer expectations to meet, and guidelines set forth by her producer. "When will you tell Molly and the staff? You'll need to close for a few days."

"They'll find out tomorrow." He tapped his fingers on the cover page. "First, I want more specifics to make sure I understand what will happen here." Jack raised his cup and continued to stare.

She held his scrutiny. Since striking out on her own, she'd never backed down from a challenge, and she wouldn't start now. "First, I need you to sign the contract, giving me permission to do the makeover." She opened the folder and handed him a pen, hoping he didn't read the boilerplate document line-by-line. "Please sign by the X."

"Give me a few more minutes. I haven't read the entire thing." Jack ran a finger along the pages, skimming the legalese created by the studio attorneys.

Sydney didn't understand half the mumbo jumbo spelled out in the contract; she only knew it gave her the right to do what she saw fit to get the restaurant back in shape.

Jack scratched his neck. "Molly is not to be on camera." He picked up the pen and scribbled a note in the side margin. "I mean it. You and your crew will not exploit my daughter, or the entire production is off."

His accusation made her tense. She had no intention of exploiting anyone. Everyone in each episode wanted to be filmed, and those who declined didn't come onto the set. Because Molly was a minor, the studio needed Jack to sign a release, which would not happen, so she'd find a solution. "I understand, Jack. We'll try to do most of our production while she's at school, or late at night, as you've seen from previous episodes."

"Good. Then you'll have no issues initialing here." Jack drew an X next to the words he'd written.

"No." Sydney didn't, but Becca might. Her producer would have to hire an actress to read Molly's letter. She placed her initials on the paper.

"Good." Jack signed his name.

Sydney breathed a sigh of relief, mingled with apprehension. This town, this man, and this restaurant made her question her life's decisions as she sat in front of the Grand Hotel's fireplace. Working together would be torture, but she owed Molly and Jack a profitable place again. Once she did, she could return to L.A., knowing she'd done her best, and assure a new contract.

"Okay. So now what?" He dropped the pen on the counter, and a frown pursed his lips.

"I go into the specifics."

He steepled his fingers under his chin and stared at the wall.

His rigid posture contradicted his aftershave, which invited her to linger in his presence.

"What happens if I don't agree?"

"You just signed the contract." She put the papers back in the folder. If he insisted, she'd destroy it and use the hotel restaurant in the hotel, but she didn't want to do that. After seeing this town and meeting several residents, she bought into Becca and Marv's vision for the Christmas special, even though she didn't buy into the Christmas hype. Using the Piñon Gulch Tavern would pacify her producers, but it wouldn't have the same impact as Joe's Café.

"Here." Disappointment swirled through her veins as she pushed the folder toward him. "I want you to be one hundred percent certain this is what you want. You know where to find me. Let me know your final decision by eight tomorrow morning. In the meantime, I'll work on my alternative plans."

****

"Cynthia said you wanted to see me?" In Jack's office three hours later, Sydney sat in the chair next to his.

Jack swiveled away from the computer screen and stared, drumming his fingers against the armrest.

"You've changed your mind about allowing me to use Joe's Café for my show and want to give me the contract."

He continued to stare.

But his expression gave her no clue as to why he requested the meeting. "You haven't changed your mind, and you want me to watch you shred the contract." She leaned forward, refusing to look away. No man would intimidate her.

A sigh escaped as he rubbed his eyes with his palms, and a pregnant pause stretched out into the tension in the air.

Finally, Jack fetched the folder containing the contract and her ideas.

He acted as if the papers contained anthrax.

"I need to do something. I checked my numbers again. Sales are decreasing, and costs are rising. I'm scraping by, and the older Molly gets, the more expensive she becomes."

Sydney squeezed his hand. Was it possible he'd come around to her way of thinking? "Jack, you've done your best. Running a restaurant is hard work. I have no experience with children, but I know from seeing my friends with kids, raising Molly alone is difficult. I imagine doing both is next to impossible. What I'll do is make this place successful so you can hire enough staff so Joe's Café will run itself." Hope flickered through his expression and softened the lines around his eyes.

"I like that idea. Every day Molly gets older, and I'm losing valuable time." Jack pulled away and took the folder from his desk.

When he stood and handed it back, she made certain she avoided touching him. "Thank you, Jack. You won't regret your decision." Sydney scraped her chair legs against the tile and hugged him. *Mistake*. The way she fit in his arms scared her, yet she didn't want to be anywhere else, and that thought terrified her more. As she gripped the front of his button-down shirt, his warmth soothed the chill in her hands. His heartbeat matched the crazy beating of her own. His breath caressed the top of her head, and for the moment, she felt safe. She could get used to this feeling as she sighed and buried herself deeper in his embrace.

What was she doing? She was here to film an episode to assure a contract renewal next year and not become involved with anyone. But she wouldn't deny she had developed feelings for Jack and his daughter.

Had she made a mistake coming to Silver Ridge?

Breaking away, she retreated to regain her professionalism. She shoved what had just transpired to the back of her mind and turned her attention on how to keep her voice from shaking. "Jack, I'm looking forward to helping you and Molly, so I need to understand more about why this place has such a special connection to you and your family. I've made a lot of notes, but the more background you provide, the more I can use that information to incorporate into the changes." Sydney collected a deep breath and exhaled. "Tell me about Marin."

****

"My late wife?" Sydney's embrace had steadied Jack, and until she broke away, he could have stood there all afternoon holding her, and inhaling her unique fragrance. He pulled together his emotions and scraped a hand through his hair for the umpteenth time that day as he sank back in his chair. Sydney had that effect on him.

"Marin and I met in first grade. We were inseparable, and we married the summer we graduated from high school. She was the daughter my parents never had, and they loved her. They died six months after our wedding, and I'm glad they didn't experience the pain of her passing." Jack rubbed his eyes, but his late wife's vision remained etched inside the darkness of his eyelids. The young, laughing Marin who'd always brought sunshine into his life.

"What happened?"

"Marin was the heart and soul of this place. When she died, all the life disappeared. I don't feel it in my bones anymore. I loved it here and wanted to be here. Joe's Café meant family, and love, and a meaningful future. Now the place is an albatross. I'm here because of Molly, and I don't know what else to do." Tears burned the back of his eyelids, and the lump in his throat made swallowing impossible. He buried his face in his hands, and his shoulders shook. Sydney's touch did little to comfort the years of accumulated pain etched into his soul.

"I wish I'd succumbed to the cancer. That I was the one who endured the pain of the exhaustive treatments, and the nausea, and the vomiting. And at the end, I was the one who wilted before my wife's eyes, knowing nothing more could be done. The waiting, the wondering, and the questions from my four-year-old daughter I had no answers for. I'm strapped because I took a loan against our house to use for Marin's treatment. Now I only have debt, fading memories, an ache in my heart, and the knowledge Molly doesn't remember her mother, despite all my efforts."

Survivor's guilt consumed him. Should he dispose of everything and move away from the ghosts? Then he wouldn't need to deal with Sydney Ryan or the pitiful glances he received from his customers and other people when he went to do errands.

"Oh, Jack. I'm so sorry."

Sydney hugged him and rested her chin against the top of his head. His body shook with unshed tears as sorrow cascaded off him like an avalanche. He stiffened but didn't shrug out of her grasp. Jack never had the chance to grieve for his wife. Maybe if what she promised turned out to be true, and the restaurant could run itself, he'd find time to mourn. Being held felt natural and right. Their hearts beat a staccato rhythm together, easing his loneliness.

He could get used to someone who cared for him again and someone to talk to. For too long he'd been the sole support for his late wife and his daughter. He'd shouldered all the responsibility then, and still did today. Sometimes late at night, he missed holding his late wife's hand. He missed their conversations. He missed her strength and compassion, her loving, and her selfless nature. Marin had told him to love again, but he'd never entertained that possibility. Three years later, he wavered.

The woman holding him was not the answer. He shrugged out of her grasp. "Her treatment was controversial, but it didn't work. Nothing did." Jack buried his face in his hands again. More unwanted moisture gathered in his eyes, but he refused to let the tears fall. Men don't cry. Jack raised his head and looked at Sydney. "Every month I pay the bills and think of the injustice. Why her? Why not me?"

He reached out to stroke her face and touch her warmth, and take her passion for his restaurant.

When she turned her cheek into his palm, her eyes filled with tears.

Leaning forward, he captured Sydney's emotions.

A knock sounded on the office door.

"Jack?"

Uncle Ray's interruption brought him to his senses.

What was he doing? He stiffened and fought the urge to caress her softness and kiss away the light, pink tint that beckoned like a candle in the window on a cold, dark night. Her unique scent drifted by his nose. She made him feel alive again, want companionship, a relationship, and a stepmom for Molly. He bit his lip and tasted blood at his disloyalty to Marin. His late wife's memory deserved better. He pushed away.

The door cracked open, and Uncle Ray appeared. "Jack, I'm heading out for the day. I've got a doctor's appointment at three."

"Thanks for the reminder. Let me know how the appointment goes. See you tomorrow." Jack rubbed his neck to keep from touching Sydney again.

"Good night, Sydney." Uncle Ray grinned.

"Good night, Ray."

Once his uncle disappeared, Jack composed himself. "I'm sorry. I didn't mean for that to happen."

"No apology necessary."

Jack heard her voice take on a huskiness as she stood and smoothed out a nonexistent wrinkle in her shirt. What had just happened? He wasn't looking for another relationship, and he suspected Sydney wasn't either.

His action scared him. The embrace only deepened whatever emotions he experienced when he was near this woman. He searched his memory for Marin's image, but the only thing he saw was Sydney Ryan's smiling face, and all he wanted was to be near her.

He stared at the paper on top of the folder containing the signed contract. Sydney's flowery handwriting reminded him of her femininity, as did her elegant neck and full, sensuous lips. The gentle way she cradled him against her softness when he broke down earlier brought out a need for companionship he'd buried along with Marin.

He didn't trust himself to keep her at arm's length, which would only lead to heartache. "I'm having second thoughts."

Sydney placed her palms flat on the desk, her lips straightening into a line.

Her eyes narrowed and flashed a fire, a passion he hadn't seen in a long time. Years ago, he wore that same expression when he looked in the mirror. Now all he saw was a defeated thirty-year-old with a struggling business and a daughter to raise alone.

"Listen, Jack, I have no clue what goes through your mind or how you feel, because I've never experienced that kind of loss. All I see is your restaurant is dying, and you're doing nothing to save it." Sydney swallowed. She glanced at the ceiling and bit her lip. "You did everything to save Marin. Do the same here before you can't."

Anger boiled his blood. How dare she? She had no right to speak Marin's name, much less compare her struggles with cancer to the issues with the restaurant. "That was a low blow." Jack hissed and pointed to the door. "Get out."

"That comment was necessary. When will you understand what you have is special? Allow me to run with it."

Only the sound of ragged breathing filled the space. Jack stared into her sympathetic, green eyes. Any words in his brain stuck in his throat. Marin was dead, leaving him to provide for Molly to the best of his ability, which hadn't been great.

Take care of our Molly. Marin's voice echoed in his mind. He scooted away his chair, needing space to think. Too bad she wouldn't distance herself.

Jack stood and paced the small confines, Sydney watching his every move. What she proposed made sense. If only he believed in the restaurant like she did. She was right; he had to do something for Molly's sake. Marin would have wanted him to have the celebrity's help. He heard Sydney playing with her necklace, zipping the charm from one side to the other.

"Is the contract still valid, Jack?"

He passed a hand over his face before he squeezed the bridge of his nose. His shoulders sagged. "I don't have a choice, do I? I signed away my life."

Sydney hugged him again.

Her perfume filled his nose again, and the warmth of her body crushed against his created tremors along his spine. The next two weeks would be torture.

****

"Hi, Becca." Sydney put her rental car in Park and tapped her fingers on the steering wheel Thursday afternoon.

"Hi, Syd."

"How are you feeling today?" Sydney eyed the few cars in the parking lot, glad to see Jack had customers. He planned to tell the staff about *Ryan to the Rescue* once the café closed, but before Molly arrived from school.

"Bloated. I can't believe I'm pregnant again."

"You are and loving every minute. How's Tabby?"

"So healthy she and her cousin, Penelope, got into my purse and had fun yesterday."

"Send me a picture. I can't wait to see." Sydney

108

laughed, imagining two three-year-olds smearing lipstick on each other's faces. Tabitha was a handful. She allowed her mind to wander to Molly, and she wondered what mischievous things Jack's daughter had done at that age. Then she remembered her mother died when she was not much older than Tabby now. She bit her lip and tried not to dwell on her thoughts with Christmas so close.

"No problem. Will do once we're off the phone. Well?"

"The signed contract is on its way."

"I knew I could count on you to get the job done. You're a professional. I expect this will be our highest-rated episode and look fantastic during the contract negotiations. Superb job."

Sydney's vocal cords refused to work. Through the window, she saw Jack talking with a customer, and a chemical reaction erupted inside. Why was this response happening? Her show and future dreams kept her busy. She'd never been lonely before or needed anyone's company, but then again, she'd met no one like Jack and Molly. She'd better get a handle on her emotions or completing the makeover would be more of a challenge than expected.

"Hello?"

Becca's word buzzed in her ear, breaking the spell. "I'm here." Sydney focused her attention on the exterior of the old railroad station.

"Okay, a change in plans. Emily arrives late Friday night; Lauren and the rest of the crew arrive late Saturday. They'll set up after the place closes Sunday, and filming starts Monday. The construction foreman said he can't paint the exterior because of the cold, so interior only, and leave the rest for the owner."

Sydney twirled a loose piece of hair. "I'll work with Emily to display Christmas decorations to draw attention from the peeling paint." Their best designer would do an amazing job to make the exterior cozy and inviting to match the interior. "Can you have Emily bring a small production T-shirt?"

"Sure thing. I—" The line went silent. "Marv's calling. I'll touch base later. Bye."

Once inside the warm café, Sydney dropped her purse on the table, removed the gloves she'd purchased yesterday, and shoved them in her pocket. Then she peeled off her coat and slung it over the back of the chair next to the window. A few customers lingered, but none of them gave her more than a cursory glance. Good. Maybe a few people in Silver Ridge didn't recognize her because a knit cap covered her loose hair. She breathed in the aroma of fresh-brewed coffee mingling with the smell of burning wood.

With no staff in sight, and as if on autopilot, she strode behind the counter and poured a cup of coffee. Being inside Joe's Café felt natural. After grabbing a small, single-serve cream container, Sydney peeled off the top and dumped the contents along with a packet of sugar into the dark liquid. Then she grabbed a spoon from the silverware tray and stirred. She made a mental note to switch to real cream served in white, porcelain containers to make a good impression on the customers.

Sydney wanted to get started. The place had good bones and only needed a strategic vision and an overhaul to bring it into the twenty-first century. As she made her way back to the table, she heard the kitchen door open.

"I'll be right there."

"No hurry, Jack." Sydney put down her coffee cup on the table and settled in a chair. She was an hour early for the staff meeting. Even though she was familiar with the restaurant, she wanted to draw a few more ideas to give to Emily. Jack wouldn't approve, but she'd deal with his displeasure when the time came.

****

The sound of chairs scraping against the tile floor caught Jack's attention once the last of the customers vacated the restaurant. Frank and Max had joined Uncle Ray, Mrs. Collins, and Sydney, choosing seats at the next table, speculation and interest written in their expressions.

Time for the staff meeting. "Thanks for staying late, everyone," Jack announced. His employees needed to understand what would happen with the makeover and how the process impacted them. Sydney would be a fixture here for however long filming took, but not only her, a whole slew of production people, cameras, and construction crews were expected. The invasion of privacy would be hard. He scratched the back of his neck. "Frank, I think you're the only one who hasn't met Sydney Ryan. Frank Moore, Sydney Ryan." Jack waved a hand. "Sydney Ryan, Frank Moore."

"Hello, Sydney." Frank raised his eyebrows, a wry grin twisting his lips. He extended his hand to Sydney.

Jack swore he saw him wink.

"Pleased to meet you. You're just as beautiful in person as you are on television. Welcome to Joe's Café."

"I'm blushing. Thanks. I'm delighted to meet you, too. I'm glad you're better." Sydney returned his smile.

111

A strange sensation overtook Jack. He should be the one holding Sydney Ryan's hand now, not his sixty-five-year-old cook. He pressed his fingertips into his eyelids. What was wrong? Jealousy and Jack Ransom didn't belong in the sentence, but when Frank dropped her hand, his symptoms eased.

Jack looked out the window and saw clouds gathering into another storm. The next two weeks promised to be long, tough holiday season in more ways than one. "Okay, this is the entire staff." He rubbed the fatigue from his eyes. He'd signed the contract, and Sydney sat there, the smile playing on her lips, making the outside world cease to exist until he blinked away the moment.

The restaurant's drab interior mocked him. No wonder business had dwindled over the years. The one person who could save it was someone who could wreak havoc with his emotions unless he locked them down. He had no choice if he wanted to leave Molly a legacy, but as soon as she finished production, Sydney would return to L.A.

He feared she'd take his heart when she left.

Chapter Eight

The chime over the front door jingled. Molly was right on time, and not a moment too soon. The meeting had finished five minutes earlier.

"Ms. Sydney!" Molly squealed. "I was hoping I'd see you again."

Her backpack hit the floor with a thud, then she ran and flung herself into Sydney's arms.

Jack's relief was short-lived. Her action hurt. Molly always greeted him when she walked through the door. "Hi to you, too, Molly. Please do your homework while I finish closing."

"Hi, Daddy. Okay." Molly darted her gaze between him and Sydney. An enormous smile split her face as she plopped on the next seat. "Why are you here?"

"I needed a cup of coffee." Sydney showed her white ceramic mug.

Jack planted himself on the wooden chair, rested his forehead against his fingertips, and rubbed at the budding headache. "Molly, I'm letting Ms. Sydney use Joe's Café for an episode of *Ryan to the Rescue*."

Molly squealed again, jumped, and twirled across the floor with outstretched hands. "Yippee! I knew you'd agree, Daddy." She came back to the table and hugged him. "Didn't I tell you he'd agree, Ms. Sydney? That means I'll get to see you every day. And not just here. We can go to the Christmas Caroling on the

Square festival together, visit Santa, eat dinner, watch movies—!"

Her reaction hurt Jack again. He needed to find time to spend with Molly. Having her get attached to Sydney meant heartache for his daughter when she finished production and returned to L.A. The woman did not belong in a small town.

Jack did his best, but it became obvious Molly craved female companionship. Should he ask his elderly neighbor to spend time with her? Unlike the TV star, Mrs. Lowell would stay in Silver Ridge. He hoped Sydney's makeover made a difference, and the place would run itself, freeing him to focus on his daughter. "Molly, there won't be any time."

"Your dad's right." Sydney agreed. "A lot goes into producing one of my episodes, but I promise we'll do something together before I leave."

Disappointment clouded his daughter's face. Just as Jack feared, Molly's growing attachment to the celebrity could only lead to heartache. The knowledge his daughter wanted to do things with Sydney she had shared with her father and mother before Marin passed away bothered him. He also vowed to do more with Molly outside of the usual traditions, starting with taking her ice skating once the outdoor rink opened.

"Okay, but I'll still see you while you're helping my dad. My friends will be jealous."

Sydney caught his gaze but remained silent.

Relief coursed through him when she didn't mention the clause he'd written into the contract. The director would film the show during Molly's school day or in the evening when she wasn't there. He'd tell his daughter in private.

A few minutes later, Jack refilled Sydney's coffee cup. Then he retrieved the gallon of milk from the refrigerator and poured Molly a glass to go along with a leftover blueberry muffin and a sliced apple. "Here. Let's move you to the table by the fireplace so you can spread out." He walked over and set down the glass and plate for his daughter. "Did you want anything, Sydney?"

"No thanks. I'm good." Coffee cup in hand, she followed Molly.

"She can eat some of mine, Daddy. Sharing is caring."

"Thanks, Molly. I'm not hungry, but I appreciate the thought."

The woman's entire face lit up when she smiled at his daughter, and he didn't blame Molly for wanting to be near her. He had the same reaction. Without thinking, he strode to the fireplace and placed another log on top to keep the place cozy until he set the alarm and locked the back door. He stretched his hands out to the warmth, instead of joining them to bask in Sydney's glow. If he wasn't careful, his emotions would get burned, too.

****

After sitting, Sydney pulled her necklace from underneath her sweater and fingered the charm on the chain. She'd found the whimsical silver owl necklace in one of the quaint vintage stores in town.

"Guess what we did today?" Molly looked at the owl charm in Sydney's fingers.

"I don't know. I wasn't there." Sydney laughed. "Why don't you tell us?"

Molly stood, skipped around the tables, and

115

flapped her arms. "Hoot. Hoot. We dissected owl pellets in science."

"Owl pellets? Sounds-um-interesting."

"And disgusting, too. We worked in groups. Rory Fisher and Ethan Boyd did the dissecting, Maggie Sloan gagged most of the time, so I drew all the pictures." Molly held out a piece of lined paper. "See all the bones and the fur."

"What is an owl pellet?" Sydney suspected by looking at the drawing, but she wanted to hear, anyway. By focusing on Molly, she didn't have to be aware Jack had stepped beside her. His nearness did crazy things inside again.

"Owls can't digest all of their prey, so it gets stuck in their gizzards and then they throw it up." Molly pretended to cough out a pellet.

The girl was a bit too animated in her description, and Sydney knew she enjoyed talking about it. Molly might be a future veterinarian or doctor if she decided to change careers. "I hope the teacher disinfects the thing." She set down her coffee cup. Talking about owl vomit made her hands feel dirty.

"I'm sure she does." Jack walked over, took the piece of paper, and stared. "Your drawing is superb, Molly. Great job."

Jack's daughter gave him a hug and an enormous smile. "Thanks, Daddy."

Sydney picked up the cup again and stared outside to give them a moment alone. She saw the snowman she, Molly, and Jack had made Sunday. Mr. White's crooked mouth created from a handful of raisins grinned back. A carrot nose and two green olives for eyes rounded out his face. Twigs Jack cut from the tree behind the restaurant served as arms, and a red and white scarf and matching hat completed the rest of his appearance. They'd decided Mr. White should face the window to brighten both their customer's and Molly's day while she did her homework. If they had a chance later, they'd build Mrs. White by the entrance to greet customers.

"Ms. Sydney, can you test me on my spelling?"

Molly's question diverted Sydney's thoughts. "Sure. If your father doesn't mind." She peeked at the man standing behind Molly. His pursed lips matched the cool expression in his eyes.

"Not at all. You can do them while I finish things in the kitchen."

His folded arms spoke of disapproval and contradicted his words. "Let me know if you need anything."

"Okay, Daddy."

When he spun on his heel and strode off, Sydney stopped herself from going after him. The man considered her a threat. No wonder he didn't want her there. A few moments later, Sydney shifted her attention back to Jack's daughter. "Let's take a look at your words."

Molly pushed the list across the desk. "You say the word and I write it. Then you check them to see if I spelled them right."

"Seems simple enough." Sydney picked up the paper. "Do the words need to be in order, or should I mix them?"

"Mix them, please. That's what Mrs. Baxter does." Molly fingered her pencil. "She says the word and then uses it in a sentence."

"That makes sense. Are you ready?"

Molly nodded.

"*Inventor*. Benjamin Franklin was an *inventor*." The sound of the pencil on paper echoed in her ears. Sydney liked the laid-back lifestyle here that contrasted the energetic and hectic pace of L.A. She'd forgotten the simpler things like a warm fire, making snow angels, and taking time to savor a good cup of coffee. After taking another sip, she looked back at the paper.

"Next, please?"

Sydney stared at the list. Who came up with these words? *Fault*? *Disappear*? And how would she use them in a sentence? Is it your dad's *fault* I can't think straight because I'm attracted? Your dad would love it if I disappeared? Why didn't the list of words have sample practice sentences next to each word? Dealing with grumpy owners, difficult makeovers, and minor setbacks she could handle. A third-grade spelling list left her dizzy and out of sorts.

"Ms. Sydney? What's the next word?"

"*Mother*." Silence stretched out. Sydney couldn't think of a sentence. The very word conjured the memory of the girl's loss.

"My *mother* is dead," Molly whispered.

"So is mine, Molly. She died when I was not much older than you are now. You're not alone." Sydney squeezed her forearm, fighting the urge to envelop the girl in a hug. Her father and uncle deserved that right.

Molly scratched the word on the paper. "*Mother*. Do you remember yours? I don't remember mine. I was really little. But my daddy says she was special."

"I know she was special. She had you as a daughter. I'm sorry you don't remember yours, though.

I do remember things about mine, but sometimes I think my memories are things I've remembered from photographs and not the real event." Sydney stared at the falling snow out the far window, the fluffy flakes drowning the gray air in a sea of white. "My mother loved me as much as yours loved you, and they still do, even though they're not here with us."

"Then why did she leave me? Why did yours leave you?" Tears filled Molly's eyes, and her bottom lip wobbled.

If the girl cried, she would join her. In her youth, Sydney struggled with the same questions herself, and she still didn't have a satisfying answer. She toyed with the owl charm again. "They didn't want to leave us, but God called them home. For reasons we don't understand, He needed them in Heaven." Sydney remembered Molly's words from the first day they met. "Look. She's thinking of you. She's helping the other angels make snow."

Molly glanced out the window before she stared at Sydney's fingers. "She is. I like your necklace, Ms. Sydney. I wish I had one like that. Owls are neat."

"I think so, too. I find something mystical about them." She fixated her attention on the flames consuming the log Jack placed on the fire earlier. Smoke filled her senses while crackling filled her ears.

Jack pulled out the opposite chair and sat next to his daughter.

The only thing that beat a roaring fire was being near Jack and Molly.

"Let me see the necklace."

He captured her gaze, and for a moment, she forgot to breathe. Why did this man have such an effect on her?

"Do you know the symbolism of the owl?"

"There is one?" She zipped the charm along the thin silver chain again, but she didn't break the thin current streaming between them.

"What is it, Daddy?" Molly popped another piece of muffin into her mouth.

"It means transition."

"Transition? What's that mean?"

Jack sipped his coffee and furrowed his brows.

"Change. An owl appears when a change is near."

"What will change for Ms. Sydney? You and I should have an owl, Daddy. Our restaurant will change. Unless…" Molly looked at Sydney.

At the child's look of longing, Sydney changed her mind. "You're right, Molly. Here." She unclasped the necklace and pushed it across the table, not knowing how many more opportunities she would have to see Jack's daughter. "It's a present."

Jack's daughter widened her eyes, and her mouth formed a perfect O.

"Thank you, Ms. Sydney. I'll treasure it forever." Molly slipped the chain over her head, grabbed the charm, and gawked. "It's so beautiful. Does this bluish color stone have meaning?"

"Turquoise is worn for protection." The shop's owner told her the symbolism of the bead between the owl and the tiny branches connecting the charm to the chain. Sydney didn't believe those words unless she needed to shield her heart.

Molly emptied her glass of milk and wiped her mouth with her blue sleeve instead of the napkin by her plate. She gasped. "Do I need protection? I'm only eight."

"Everyone does." Sydney didn't miss Jack's glance before focusing on his daughter. His fear Molly would get too close and be hurt when she left might be justified. She was getting attached to Jack's daughter, too.

Nothing good could come of this bond. She was glad Molly wouldn't be in the restaurant during production, because the young girl with the crystal blue eyes and ready smile had already staked a claim on her heart just like her father.

Sydney needed to remember her life was in L.A. She'd negotiate a new contract early next year, moving her dream of owning her own restaurant closer, and in a few short weeks she'd be lying on the beach in the Caymans, sipping an exotic cocktail without a care in the world.

****

"What did you make?" Jack questioned.

He flipped his gaze between Sydney and the five plates she garnished in the prep area Friday afternoon. She knew the town buzzed, and according to Mrs. Collins, people who hadn't been inside Joe's Café for years stopped by to glimpse the celebrity in their midst. While Jack helped Mrs. Collins out front, Sydney stepped in behind the line. With Frank out again, Uncle Ray struggled to fill the orders and extra special items.

As much as she liked and respected the old man, she realized he was part of the problem because he couldn't keep up with the orders. Sydney swallowed. She would work with him on timing. "Lunch. Tacos with goat cheese and fresh chips and salsa." She crossed her fingers behind her back. She wasn't lying because she had made tacos. She just hadn't disclosed all ingredients and hoped Jack wouldn't ask before he took a bite. "Will you help me take them to the counter?"

Jack glanced between her and the plates. "You don't need to cook for us. We fend for ourselves. Sunday was an anomaly."

Sydney conjured up a sweet smile. "I thought we could put tacos on the lunch menu."

He furrowed his brow and pursed his lips. "You were to run everything by me, first."

"I am. Here you go." Sydney grabbed two plates. "I can't wait to hear everyone's thoughts."

Once seated at the counter, Sydney bit into her concoction. She'd never made a vegetarian taco, but the few tastes she'd sampled while cooking hadn't been too bad. The additional garlic added another dimension to the flavor as did the homemade salsa. Next time, she'd put black beans on the plate for color and add small white ramekins for the salsa and guacamole to improve the presentation.

When Jack took a bite and chewed, he pulled his eyebrows together and cocked his head as he looked inside the taco. "Interesting, but I don't recognize the protein base. What's inside?" He searched the contents.

"I don't either, but I love the taste." Suzette nodded. "Especially the homemade chips and salsa. Sydney, do you know how to make a good breakfast burrito? I've had customers ask over the past few months."

"I can incorporate that entrée into the new menu, for your customers." Sydney dabbed her mouth with a napkin. "As for your question, Jack, I'll give you a hint.

The protein comes in a white and green package."

Jack coughed and reached for his water.

To avoid laughing, she clamped her teeth. At least he didn't spit out her creation.

He wrinkled his nose and pursed his lips. "I said no tofu."

"I couldn't resist. Like I said before, tofu has its place in American cuisine." Sydney grinned.

"Not in here." Jack pushed away his plate. "Leave your hippie mumbo jumbo in L.A. where it belongs."

Sydney wedged her hands against her hips and pursed her forehead. "Almost every ingredient can be used in something else, so it wouldn't go to waste if the customers don't like it."

"No." Jack growled and crushed his napkin.

"Try it, Jackson." Uncle Ray set down his half-eaten taco and wiped his mouth. "Customers like the new menu items except for Mr. Withers, but nothing makes the old man happy."

"Your customer base is changing." Sydney gestured toward the empty dining area. "People are looking for healthier alternatives and are removing meat and chicken from their diets. Offer them another choice besides meat and potatoes or they won't come back."

"She's right." Suzette stood and smoothed out her apron. "I've kept my mouth shut over the years. Keep with the times, Jack. You've agreed to let Sydney make over Joe's Café. Let her. Your way isn't working anymore. Unless things change, you'll be out of business, and I'll have to find another job."

Color drained from his face and white shrouded his pursed lips. For a moment, she thought she saw a sheen in his eyes, but he blinked away the tears and rested his forehead against his palms. Sydney's heart went out, because she knew he didn't want her or her ideas there, but she, Uncle Ray, and Suzette spoke the truth. She needed to do the show her way. Once she returned to L.A., he could change things, but for his and Molly's sake, she hoped he didn't. He had to get customers in the door and keep them coming back.

Jack banged a fist on the counter. "Fine. You win again, *Ms. Ryan*. I hope I can relate to Joe's Café once you're done."

When she saw Jack pull back his plate and pick up a chip, she almost jumped out of her seat.

"What? I'm hungry. Looks like I have to get used to this food, anyway."

She grinned at her small victory. One small step for Jack. One giant leap for Sydney.

****

"Do you have a few minutes?" Jack questioned.

Sydney looked from her notes to see him standing next to the chair in the hotel lobby where she'd been enjoying another afternoon cup of tea by the fire. She removed her socked feet from the ottoman and sat straighter. His white-knuckled grip on his hat belied any sense of calm as she motioned for him to sit. The gingerbread cookie eaten an hour ago churned in her stomach. What now? "Sure. Have a seat."

Only piped-in Christmas music and the muted sounds of other conversations hung in the air as Jack filled the next chair. Despite the surrounding activity, they were the only two in the room as they shared a moment gazing into each other's eyes. Sydney forgot to breathe as her heartbeat accelerated.

"I want to apologize for my behavior these past couple of days." Jack sighed and thrust a hand through his hair. "I've never behaved in such a poor manner to a complete stranger before."

She squeezed his forearm resting on the armrest. As expected, a tangible energy coursed through her and zapped her nerves. Why did this man make her blush like a schoolgirl? She focused on his words and smiled. "I'm not a complete stranger. You let me into your living room once a week."

A slight grin twisted his mouth, and he gazed out the window on the right side of the fireplace. "True. Should I change that to a customer? I've never acted that way before, not even with old man Withers, and he can be trying."

She followed his gaze. The Christmas lights wrapped around the wrought iron light pole cast a warm glow on the fresh snow. The bright red bow danced in the light breeze, forecasting more precipitation tomorrow. She hoped her crew didn't have any trouble getting into town tomorrow night. Emily was due tonight, but she decided to stay in Denver overnight and would arrive in the morning. "For reasons we don't understand, Jack, I bring out the worst in you. Your reluctance to change must be because you think you're betraying your family's heritage, but change is necessary. I promise I'll try and keep the integrity of what your grandparents started."

Jack shut his eyes and squeezed the bridge of his nose. "My late wife was the heart and soul of Joe's Café. We talked a lot about what we wanted to do and our hopes and dreams, as I imagined my grandparents and parents did."

"So, you're betraying her memories because I'm making the changes." Sydney sensed his unrest as he rubbed his eyes.

"Marin told me to use the life insurance money to fix the place. I couldn't do it without her, so I used it to pay the uncovered medical bills."

Sydney stared at their entwined fingers and wondered who initiated the contact. Sitting here, holding Jack's hand, and talking about the restaurant felt so natural. Her grip tightened. "I'm sorry about Marin. Will you share your plans? I'll see if we can incorporate them into my vision."

Jack tensed and caught her gaze. Lines creased his forehead.

She fought the instinct to touch his face.

"They weren't much. We had more love than money, but Marin always wanted to go through the attic because she thought the boxes my grandparents stored there for decades would contain a goldmine of information. Once the restaurant closes tomorrow afternoon, I'd like to look."

"I'm sure Molly would enjoy herself. My designer will be here, too, so if we find anything, Emily will know what to do." Contented, Sydney stared at the fire again. Who knew holding Jack's hand created such a simple pleasure. "I find something comforting about the orange glow, the comfy smell of burning wood, and the Christmas decorations that make me feel like I've come home."

"Silver Ridge ambience." The lines in his face softened, and his lips curved upward as a faraway expression clouded his eyes. "People leave but always come back. Take my Uncle Ray, for example."

"Excuse me," a girl's voice interrupted. "Are you Sydney Ryan of *Ryan to the Rescue*?"

Jack pulled away.

The moment disappeared. She felt adrift and incomplete. Sydney was used to the attention, and she'd do well to remember her time in Silver Ridge was limited to the production schedule. By Christmas, she'd be on the beach relaxing, and Jack would be the owner of a successful restaurant.

She studied the high school teenager who had broken off from a group of giggling girls standing on the other side of the Christmas tree. From appearances, her friends dared her to approach. She grinned at the one brave enough to talk. "Who's asking?"

"Whitney Horton." Bright red burst across the girl's cheeks as she toed her sneaker into the floor.

"I am, Whitney Horton, and I like your spunk. You'll do well in life."

Whitney pulled out her smart phone. "Thanks? Um, can I take a picture with you?"

"Of course." Sydney stood and motioned for the girl to move in next to the chair. Three photos later, she grinned and took her seat again. "If your friends want one, too, then they have to ask."

"Thanks, Ms. Ryan. You are so cool." The girl retreated, and the group jostled their way out the front door.

"That's Molly in a few years." Jack sighed as he placed his elbows on his knees and rested his chin on his steepled fingers. "I'm not ready."

"No parent is. I hear at that age most of them think their teenager is from another planet." Sydney glanced around the semi-crowded lobby, searching for another familiar face but came up empty. "Where's Molly?"

"She's spending the night with her friend, Sam."
Jack stood and held out a hand. "I'm hungry. We've
called a truce, so let's grab a bite to eat. Since we'll be
seeing a lot of each other for the next few weeks, we
should get to know each other better."

"That's unnecessary." Sydney hesitated. Working
together would be a challenge during the renovation, so
spending more time outside of work was not a good
idea. She was already falling for him and his daughter.

Chapter Nine

"Dinner is necessary. Come on. We'll walk through town first. It'll be fun. I promise."

A rare smile split Jack's lips, and from the few things she'd learned over the past few days, she understood how Marin fell in love. She stopped herself from pushing away the stray curl falling across his forehead.

"If you say so, then I accept." Shrugging off her earlier thoughts, Sydney accepted his proffered arm, not surprised at the jolt of energy again. What was it about this man that set her heart fluttering?

"This way."

Once Sydney put on her shoes, jacket, and gloves, she let Jack escort her out the front door. With their footsteps muffled by the new fallen snow, and her arm tucked in his as they walked the lane that ran alongside the hotel, she found comfort.

Flakes dusted the benches lining the cobblestone walkway. Tall pine trees lit with hundreds of tiny white, red, and green lights stood like soldiers guarding the palace. A few more snowflakes fell, adding to the romantic atmosphere. White light spilled out from underneath the dark green awnings over the store windows in the red brick buildings. More holiday decorations graced the window dressings inside, complementing the garland, lights, and red ribbons anchored to the exterior panes.

Molly was right. Magic wove a spell of Christmas spirit this time of the year, and Sydney was glad to be here. "Everything here is so different from Christmas in California."

Jack chuckled and patted her arm. "I imagine. All sunshine and beach with no snow."

"Pretty much. Like the rest of the country, people put out lights and decorations, and only the houses and trees look a little different. I always laughed at the Christmas cards portraying Santa in shorts, sitting on the beach under a decorated palm tree, and drinking a margarita. That vision sums up everything." When Sydney laughed, she saw her breath. Another snowflake drifted past her vision. How different her life was this year, and she realized she wouldn't change a thing.

"I like a white Christmas."

"I've never experienced snow living in California." But then again, she hadn't spent Christmas in L.A. for years, always choosing an exotic location so she didn't have to face her childhood memories. Enough. She shrugged off the sadness struggling to grab hold of her emotions. Each passing day put more space between today and her previous experiences. She stopped in front of a window display filled with numerous bottles of balsamic vinegars and olive oils. "I suppose you order your oils and vinegars from a supplier, don't you?"

"I have little use for gourmet items." Jack used his free hand to scratch the back of his neck.

She heard him sigh as he waved to the elderly woman behind the counter.

"What are you thinking? The owner, Evelyn, has

tried to sell to me for years. I can set up a wholesale account."

Her world brightened when he agreed with her suggestion. This concession was only the start. "Five gallons of extra virgin olive oil and a gallon of balsamic vinegar, and I'll need to see which of the infused oils and vinegars she has in stock. I try to use local items to help other businesses because I like to think I'm not only rescuing a restaurant, but other places in town, too." She knew he didn't want her there, or her changes, and she had to prove he hadn't made a mistake.

"I'll call her tomorrow."

"Thanks. I appreciate that." A few moments later, she followed Jack's lead and moved on after two rambunctious kids ran by, followed by their harried parents. The little girl with the chubby red cheeks reminded her of Tabitha and what Molly probably looked like at that age. Molly, that sweet child, had wormed her way into Sydney's heart, and she couldn't wait to build another snowman, create a snow angel, or have another snowball fight. Would Jack let his daughter bake chocolate chip macadamia nut cookies with her to leave out for Santa on his big night?

She walked in a companionable silence for a few moments before stopping in front of the window of a store selling hand-knit items. Next to the nativity display, a bright and colorful scarf and mitten set lay on the side table. The perfect gift for Molly. She wondered what other stores held treasures for her in this quaint town.

Jack cleared his throat. "What do you do for the holidays in L.A.?"

"I'm always elsewhere. This year I'll be in the Caymans. Last year was Maui, and New Zealand the year before."

Jack's eyes darkened to cobalt, and a frown hugged his lips. Compassion and something she couldn't identify eased its way into his expression.

He pulled off his glove and ran his fingers along her cheek.

His touch left a trail of warmth on her skin.

"Sounds to me like you're running away."

"No more than anyone else." Sydney blinked and stepped back to break the tie holding them together. Kissing the man was not in her evening plans.

A few minutes later, Jack opened the old wood door to the Copper Bistro and ushered Sydney inside. The cozy interior blazed with life and energy. *Magic.* As he cradled her arm, she'd have never guessed she'd be dining with the handsome man giving his name at the hostess station.

In a moment, Jack and Sydney followed the teenage girl dressed in blue jeans and a green button-down shirt to their table by the window at the far end of the room. Soft tangerine paint covered the walls, complementing the light ceiling divided with dark brown timber beams. The same wood also outlined the oversized windows. White pendant lights hung from the ceiling, and old, small black-and-white hexagon tiles graced the floor. Blue votive candles in glass containers sat in the center of each table covered with white tablecloths. Folded napkins completed the upscale atmosphere. Quaint.

Jack pulled out her wood chair, eased the coat from her shoulders, and then folded it over the back of the chair. Then she watched him shrug out of his jacket and set it over hers before sliding into his seat. Sydney's heartbeat raced, and moisture fled from her mouth. Chivalry stilled existed. Men were different here, or she hadn't dated the right kind back home, which wasn't often because of her schedule.

"Nicole will be your server tonight. Can I start you off with anything?" The hostess handed them each a menu.

"Water and an iced tea for me. Sydney?"

"I'll have the same, please." She glanced at the cream-colored linen paper attached to a thin strip of wood. "The menu presentation here has a rustic charm and an old-fashioned appeal. Something similar at your place would work."

"Too upscale and impractical. The rotisserie chicken is good." He unrolled his silverware and set the linen napkin across his lap.

Jack's attitude bothered her. She didn't agree. Her ideas incorporated trends from the twenty-first century, not the 1970s. Watching him sign the contract, she'd expected pushback, but not over all her suggestions. Well, he was in for a surprise. The paperwork allowed her to do everything necessary to appeal to the viewers and adhere to the network guidelines. Sydney also understood his position, and she'd work with him as much as possible.

"I disagree. Laminated menus don't allow for simple updates. By doing it this way, you can change the menu as often as you like. See?" Sydney pulled the paper from the elastic straps and then put it back. "All you need to do is to print off new copies, which will be cheaper in the long run. When was the last time you updated your menu?" She set down the menu and tucked her napkin onto her lap.

"Last year. I didn't create a new one though. I wrote on blank, cut-up labels to change a few prices."

Light from the candle cast shadows across his strong and stubborn jawline. Well, she could be just as stubborn. "I noticed, and so did your customers, case in point. How's the Caesar salad?"

"The answer is no, and I don't know. I've never tried the salad. Molly likes the hamburgers, and I prefer a good steak. Are you a vegetarian?" Jack folded his hands and rested them on the menu, his eyebrows drawn together.

"No. Sometimes I prefer lighter fare. All I've been doing this past week is eating. So, let me guess, no new menu concept, no linen napkins, and no tablecloths."

His eyebrows rose a fraction. "Why would I consider a linen service? Paper napkins are fine and less work for the staff. We've always done it that way."

Jack aggravated her. Sydney filled her lungs and shook her head as she stared at the black-and-white photo hung on the red brick wall of eight miners standing in front of a mine. She kept her voice low even though she wanted to shout some sense into the man. "Doing things the same isn't always the right way. You've got to compete with the other restaurants in this town. Match your competition or close the place."

"A diner can use paper." Jack gestured around him. "A place like this one would use cloth."

"My point exactly. The look I'm envisioning is along these lines. More upscale. More, more this atmosphere." She opened her arms to encompass the surrounding room. The air of elegance from the linen napkins to the candles to the décor was what Sydney wanted to incorporate at Joe's Café. "When will you realize your restaurant has so much potential?"

Jack crossed his arms. "The answer is still no."

"Well, look who's eating with us tonight," a female voice interrupted.

A woman in her mid-thirties with blonde hair tied back on a loose ponytail, dressed in a bright red dress, set down two glasses of water and iced tea. She glanced between Sydney and Jack, a smile playing on her red lips.

"Nicole will be right with you to take your orders, but I had to see for myself. Where's your usual date, Jack?"

"Hi, Donna. Molly's spending the night with a friend." Jack coughed on a sip of water. "This isn't a date. Sydney Ryan meet Donna Smith. Donna Smith meet Sydney Ryan."

The woman raised her eyebrows, put out a hand, and smiled. "Hi, Sydney. Nice to meet you. You look so different in person." Instant red filled her cheeks. "I mean-I-I heard you're filming an episode at Joe's Café. My husband and I think that's a terrific idea and can't wait to see what you do with the place." The words tumbled from her mouth.

Ignoring the effect her celebrity status had on others, Sydney grinned and shook her hand. She'd heard that comment before and would again. "Thanks. It's nice to meet you, too." She could get used to the warmth and friendliness from the town's inhabitants. "Before you ask, your décor is perfect, and your menu appears to be spot on with your clientele. From all appearances, I bet you have a wait on Friday and

Saturday nights, so I wouldn't change a thing."

"Why, thank you." Donna clasped her hands and darted her gaze to Jack. Another smile created laugh lines. "Duty calls. Thanks for dining with us."

Sydney didn't attempt to decipher the woman's expression. While Jack's closeness affected her equilibrium, she was only here to bring his restaurant from the brink of extinction and film the episode that guaranteed her a new contract. She had no time or energy for a relationship.

****

Jack finished his steak and potatoes and waited. Why did women eat so slow? He'd noticed it with his mother, his late wife, his daughter, his customers, and now Sydney. Even with their light banter, he'd cleaned his plate before her and tried to ignore the graceful way she held her fork or dabbed her napkin against her lips. She also had a positive effect on the surrounding diners and the poor busboy who almost dropped the water pitcher when he refilled her glass.

"The salad was exceptional." She pushed away her plate and glanced at Jack.

"The owners do a great job here. I've heard no complaints. Would you like dessert or coffee?"

Sydney placed her elbows on the table, clasped her hands together, and rested her chin against her knuckles as she stared. "No, thanks. I'm finished."

He signaled for the check. Even though he didn't have to worry about Molly tonight, he wanted to end what Donna and a few other diners apparently considered a date. Dinner wasn't anything more than two adults eating together instead of alone. So what if he paid the tab? He'd consider it a payback for the shifts she worked and refused payment.

After guiding Sydney through the restaurant, Jack opened the door and ushered her outside. He saw her shiver. The temperature had dropped, and he suspected she wasn't used to the cold. The idea of sitting close by the hotel fire with a mug of hot chocolate sounded enticing. He took in the way her coat fit her trim body. Wrong. He pulled away, dug his hands into his pockets, and stepped onto the sidewalk.

In front of the restaurant, a large brown and white horse stood hitched to a sleigh decorated with lights and garland. A cozy, black-and-red-checked blanket rested over the back of the black leather seats.

"Oh, I've always wanted to ride in a sleigh. I've only seen them in the movies."

"The sleighs are here on the weekends in the winter, and the buggies are used all week during the summer. I've never ridden in one though. It's a tourist thing."

"I can understand. Believe it or not, I've never been to the Hollywood Walk of Fame or taken a star tour." Sydney stopped and petted the horse's head. He nudged her hand. "Sorry, buddy. Nothing for you."

"Hi, Jack." The elderly man with white hair and beard standing by the lamppost nodded.

Dressed in a dapper, long, gray jacket and matching wool bowler, the man could have stepped out of another era. Jack knew his costume was the part of the appeal. "Hi, Tom. Let me introduce you to Sydney Ryan."

"Pleased to meet you, Sydney Ryan. Your smile is like a beacon on a dark and stormy night." He kissed her hand.

Her grin widened, and she smothered a laugh.

Jack shifted.

"Likewise, Tom. Your words of flattery are music to my ears and sustenance to my soul." Sydney pulled away her hand.

Tom followed her curtsey with a bow. "Let me take you for a ride."

"We really can't, Tom. Thank you though." Jack grumbled. Why did men act like lovesick fools near Sydney? Because they recognized what he'd been ignoring. Sydney Ryan was stunning, smart, and friendly, and he was falling for her charms like every other man in Silver Ridge. The night couldn't end soon enough.

"The ride is on the house. Apollo is getting restless, and you will drum up business. Give me a cup of coffee next time I'm in. My lady?" He held out a hand and helped Sydney into the sleigh.

"Thank you."

She graced the older man with a smile Jack wanted for himself. If he didn't know better, he'd say he was jealous, but that meant he cared, which he didn't. After stepping onto the running board, he catapulted himself into the sleigh and folded his lanky body onto the seat next to Sydney. Then he settled the blanket over their legs to block out the cold. When his thigh accidently touched hers in the small area, he started to sweat. Why weren't these interiors bigger? Of course, the owners had developed the ride around romance, as seen by another couple cuddling in the sleigh passing by. Jack tugged at his collar as Tom snapped the reins.

Apollo stepped away from the blazing lights of the restaurant.

The intimate, cozy atmosphere complemented by the Christmas decorations and snow did not go unnoticed. Was Tom playing matchmaker? What about a few of his other customers who had taken a sudden interest in his life? Why couldn't he focus on his surroundings when Sydney's floral perfume drifted under his nose? He grew up in this town, and yet his memory blanked on the street names, the town's history, and why he'd been against the sleigh ride.

Without thinking, he stretched an arm across the back of the sleigh and settled across Sydney's shoulders. He drew her close, but only to keep her warm, and nothing else. So why did he enjoy holding her? Why did he want her to rest her head against his shoulder and snuggle deeper into his embrace? Why was he thinking these thoughts when Sydney Ryan was bent on disrupting his way of life?

The steady clop of the horse's hooves against the cobblestones added another dimension to their surroundings, and Jack fought to shake off the sense of compatibility. He and Sydney mixed like oil and water, or milk and orange juice, or baking soda and vinegar, as he'd discovered when helping with Molly's volcano science project. Still, he held her until the sleigh pulled in front of the hotel's entrance.

"I hope you enjoyed yourself, Sydney." Tom dipped his hat. "Any time you want another ride, let me know. Good luck with the renovation. We can't wait to see the result." Tom kissed the back of her hand again.

He held it there longer than Jack deemed necessary, and more jealousy waged war inside him. He had no claim on Sydney or anyone, and it would remain that way.

Silence hovered like an unwelcome review and accompanied him as he ascended the stairs. Jack didn't want to end the night or let her go. With Molly at Sam's house, the four walls of his bungalow would press in, reminding him of how empty his life had become.

Sydney Ryan wasn't the answer. Her presence only brought his problem to light. Plenty of single women his age, like Nadine Boyd, would love to date him, if the chance arose. All he had to do was ask or have Mrs. Collins spread the word.

He shuddered, but not from the cold. Women from Silver Ridge didn't interest him. Only the tall, leggy blonde from L.A., who was about to turn his world upside down, captured his attention.

Fear darkened his mood and twisted his emotions into a pretzel. He yanked off his glove and cradled her face in his palm, allowing the warmth of her skin to sear his. Her eyes softened to a field of green grass, and her lips parted. Enticed, he brushed his mouth against hers, only to deepen the kiss when she wrapped her arms around his shoulders.

A tiny sigh escaped her lips, inviting him to explore further. He pulled her closer, devouring her caresses. He hadn't shared such intimacy in three, long years. Disloyalty to Marin stabbed his heart. What was he doing? He stepped away. "I'm sorry. That kiss should have never happened." His breathing uneven, Jack shoved his hand back into his glove. Her touch felt so right…as if she belonged in his arms. Working with her every day until production wrapped would be torture.

"Agreed." Sydney adjusted her collar. "Thanks for dinner. Good night. See you tomorrow."

Even in the dim light, he noticed the color had drained from her face. What had he done?

Jack stared into the muted darkness long after she disappeared into the hotel. Fool. Instead of answering his question, the kiss only intensified his budding feelings. That was a position he never wanted to find himself in again.

Chapter Ten

"Good morning, Emily." Sydney hugged the short, dark-haired woman bundled in a blue parka, scarf, and hat in the hotel's lobby late Saturday morning. She was excited to show her designer Joe's Café and find out if Emily's design opinion matched her own vision.

"Morning, Sydney." The woman scanned the area. "This place is incredible. The town is so quaint and right out of a romance movie. Now I know why Marv and Becca wanted a production here. I can't wait to see the rest."

"It's magical here. How was the drive?"

"Not too bad, and perfect timing. I grew up near Denver, so my parents were ecstatic I spent last night with them and am taking off a few days postproduction to visit before Christmas." Her mouth dropped open, and her forehead wrinkled. "I can't believe I've never heard of this town."

"That's right. You're from Aurora. I'm glad you're able to spend time with your family." Sydney smiled and held out a room key. "You're checked in, so get settled and when you're ready, we'll grab a bite to eat and go over the preliminaries."

Emily took the key. "Sounds good. Let me drop off my suitcase. I can't wait to start."

Five minutes later, Sydney ushered Emily into a chair at her favorite window table in Joe's Café.

Outside the snowman, Mr. White, now joined by Mrs. White, smiled. Maybe later, she and Molly could build a few snow children to complete the family.

"Hi, Ms. Sydney." Molly skipped to their table. "The usual?"

She eyed the girl wearing a white apron over a red, long-sleeved shirt and jeans. "Yes, and a few menus, too. Molly, I'd like to introduce Emily Erikson, the designer who will make this place look fabulous. Emily, this is Mary-Katerina Quinn, or Molly, for short."

Molly held out a hand. "Pleased to meet you, Ms. Erikson. I can't wait to see what you do here, just like what you did with all the other restaurants." She leaned in and whispered into Emily's ear, "My daddy and I watch *Ryan to the Rescue* every week. I can't believe Ms. Sydney is here, and I'll be the first in my class to be on TV. The other kids are so jealous."

When Sydney overheard Molly's words, her heart plummeted. Jack hadn't told his daughter yet. She placed a finger on her lips and shook her head.

The designer winked.

"Call me Ms. Emily, and yes, she's here, Molly. Thanks to you, this episode will be the best one ever. Hey, I have a present for you." Emily pulled a white T-shirt from her bag. "Ms. Sydney asked me to bring this for you."

"My *Ryan to the Rescue* T-shirt." Molly squealed and jumped up and down as she held up her gift, revealing a picture of Sydney dressed in her white chef's jacket and a yellow hard hat, holding a wooden spoon in one hand and a hammer in the other. "Thanks, Ms. Emily. Thanks, Ms. Sydney." Molly hugged

Sydney. "I can't wait to show Sam."

"Where's Mrs. Collins?" Sydney redirected Molly's attention. She understood Jack's need to keep his daughter away from the limelight, but why did he continue to let her believe she'd be part of the production?

"We ran out of a few things, so Daddy sent her to the store. He's in the kitchen. Did you want to see him?"

"That's okay." It would be easier to discuss things without his presence. "I'll have a cup of coffee for now. Emily?"

"I'll have coffee, too, and the chicken sandwich." Emily handed Molly her menu.

Molly skipped toward the kitchen.

Emily pulled out a notepad. "She's precious. I know why you want to help."

"She is." Sydney retrieved her own notes. She was falling in love with Molly, and that wasn't good since she would leave town after she finished filming.

The designer studied the room. "I see the potential, but Joe's Café is worse than you described. How has it stayed in business?"

"I don't know. The food is mediocre, so I have a lot of work to do in the kitchen. The only thing that has saved this place is its uniqueness. We've got other considerations, though." Sydney explained about the family history of Joe's Café.

Molly placed their drinks on the table. "Here you go."

"Thanks, Molly," Sydney and Emily spoke at the same time.

"We'll need to paint and hang wallpaper on the

wall behind the fireplace." Emily dumped an open packet of sugar into her drink and studied the floor. "At least the tile is in good shape."

Scanning her notes, Sydney sipped the coffee and let the dark roast tickle her taste buds. Jack's brew was the best thing in the place. "You read my mind. I looked for pictures of the original colors at the local museum, but I only found black and white, so we'll need a new a color scheme. What about the lighting?"

Emily glanced around the room. "We're in a former train depot so we should bring that theme back to life. I want to find old lamps to use as pendant lights for the counter area, five or six old-fashioned wall sconces, and two chandeliers to brighten the center of the room."

"I like that idea." Sydney nodded. "What about the atmosphere? Let's find some old town and train depot photos to hang between antique mining equipment for wall decorations."

"Works for me. Votive candles on the tables and more on the fireplace mantel would add a nice, cozy touch along with a bouquet of flowers."

Excitement welled when Sydney envisioned the new interior in her mind's eye. "We can add a bud vase with a single flower to each table to complement the one on the mantel and place another bouquet on the bar. That should match the caliber of food I'm proposing for the kitchen."

"Ladies?" Jack materialized, carrying two plates.

"Here, Ms. Sydney. I had Daddy make you a grilled cheese sandwich like mine." Molly put two plates on the table with the sandwich and fries and grabbed a bottle of ketchup from her apron pocket.

"Your chicken sandwich." Jack set the plate in front of Emily and a burger for himself. His expression neutral, he pulled out the fourth chair opposite Sydney.

She sensed an undercurrent as he held out a hand to Emily.

"I'm Jack Ransom, the owner."

Emily paused a second before she grasped his hand and smiled.

Did her designer giggle?

"Emily Erikson." Her lips parted slightly. "Pleased to meet you, Jack Ransom. Thanks for lunch. We were discussing ideas about the interior." Pink touched her cheeks as she rushed her words. "We can't do much with the exterior because of the weather, but I'll decorate it for Christmas to draw the attention from the faded paint."

As Sydney breathed in, she clamped her pen. She'd never seen Emily babble, but then again, she wasn't immune to Jack's charm either. Her cheeks warmed at the thought of the kiss they'd shared last night.

"Decorations are upstairs in the attic." Jack dumped ketchup on his burger.

"I'll take a peek, but I have plenty of money in the budget for new ones." She bit into her sandwich.

Sydney caught the subtle shift of Emily's eyebrows as she chewed. She should use that dish as an example and create a better, more flavorful replacement for the menu which didn't include a frozen, pre-made patty.

"Sydney and I went over a few things, but we need to discuss more. We usually don't involve the owner in the design process, but I understand this case is special."

"I'll help too, right, Daddy?" Molly dipped her fry

into the mound of ketchup on her plate.

"This is a family decision." Jack nodded at his daughter.

Molly blossomed under Jack's attention, and Sydney was glad Jack included her, since the entire thing was his daughter's idea. The same with the grilled cheese sandwich, which was one of the better items that came out of the kitchen. She bit into the buttery toasted bread hiding the gooey cheesy center.

"Let's listen to what the ladies have to say after we eat, and then we'll give our input." Jack tweaked Molly's nose.

A few minutes later, Emily pushed away her half-eaten lunch and scribbled in her notepad. "First, your tables are old and worn, and your vinyl chairs are outdated. So are the barstools. Everything needs to be replaced."

"The furniture is still good," Jack growled.

Emily sat straighter and glanced at her.

Sydney warned her designer Jack was a difficult owner. Sometimes she had to pinch herself to remind herself he'd agreed to the makeover. This episode stood to be the best one done to date, which would assure her of a new contract and pay raise. "We have a generous budget on this production, Jack, and an extensive list of companies that donate their goods and services for brand recognition and a credit on my show. Replacing everything won't be an issue."

Molly tugged at Jack's sleeve. "Can we put tablecloths on the new tables like Mrs. Langley does across the street, Daddy? And napkins folded into swans? I saw that once in a movie."

Jack shook his head. "The tables are fine. Linens

require a rental service, which isn't in my budget."

Sydney clenched her coffee cup to keep from reaching out to stroke the frown from Jack's face. The man refused to understand and see the importance of what the makeover would do. "Don't forget you'll have more revenue which will more than offset the additional cost."

"How about placemats?"

Emily didn't miss a beat as Sydney watched her go over the railroad crossing sign she'd doodled.

"Tacky. We used paper ones when my parents were alive." Jack waved his hand.

"I envisioned woven vinyl ones, which are durable, elegant, and will add another dimension if you won't consider tablecloths." Emily pushed her drawing toward Jack. "Have you ever considered changing the name?"

"What's wrong with Joe's Café?" Jack growled.

"Sydney and I think you should use a name that better reflects the train depot. A creative name like the R&R Café." Emily pointed to an abstract drawing on the paper.

Jack sat back in his chair and crossed his arms. "You and Sydney?"

His expression closed again, signaling to Sydney he didn't appreciate the conversation. She should have told Emily Jack would nix the name and not mention it. Décor and menu updates and filming the final episode of the year was enough satisfaction.

"Well, the idea is Sydney's, but she can't draw so I thought of this type of logo." Emily tapped the paper again.

Sydney wanted to kick her designer, but with her

luck, she'd hit Jack instead.

"It could symbolize a few things. Sydney and I agree the interior should resemble the original train depot. You could use the railroad crossing sign with the word *café* written underneath. Each R would represent Ransom. One for you and one for Molly. It could also symbolize rest and relaxation because that's what people want when they dine out." Emily continued.

As he rose from his chair, Jack squeezed the bridge of his nose and shook his head. "Everyone in town knows Joe's Café. The name stays in honor of my grandfather. Come on, Molly. Mrs. Collins is back, so let's clean up." He turned to face Sydney, his expression dark. "All this place needs is a fresh coat of paint and different pictures. Make a list of items you're considering for the menu, the equipment you want to install, and the initial design ideas for approval." Jack spun on his heel and strode away.

Sinking back in her chair, Sydney sighed. "That didn't go well."

"Not at all. Wow." Emily's eyebrows rose, and she widened her eyes. "I've never seen an owner so reluctant to change or so resistant to our ideas. How did you convince him to do the makeover?" She bit the end of her pen.

"Persistence. I wouldn't accept no for an answer."

Emily laughed. "Sounds like you. What do we do? Everyone else arrives tomorrow."

Sydney knew when the rest of the crew arrived and what time filming started. "Have I ever disappointed any of you?"

"No, but this one will take a miracle to pull off."

She nodded. "How much time do you need to get

everything ordered and delivered?"

"You mentioned sorting through boxes in the attic. Once that's done, I'll look through the sponsoring companies' websites for what we discussed. Delivery will take a few days, making that the biggest time-delay. The crew will paint the interior and put in the new lighting and fixtures while I scour local stores for decorations. Are you sure we should continue? Jack won't be happy."

"I don't see any other option. He signed the contract, giving me free rein. I'll incorporate as many of his and his late wife's visions as I can, but to do it right, I have to go big. Sticking with his strict constraints won't work for me or the network, and I think deep down he knows that."

For the first time in her career, she had doubts about completing a project. If she wasn't doing the remodel for Molly, she'd be on the next plane out of town because anticipating the expression on Jack's face during the reveal filled her with dread.

****

"Come on, Ms. Sydney, Ms. Emily, let's go. The attic is full of boxes and stuff." Molly tugged Sydney's hand on Saturday afternoon.

The young girl pulled her toward the office, her excitement contagious.

"Shouldn't we wait for your father?" Emily paused.

Jack nodded as he counted the cash in the register. "Go ahead. I'll be there soon."

Sydney couldn't shake the emotions Jack evoked with a kiss that shouldn't have happened, but did, and she couldn't forget it. His caress had turned her insides and brain into mashed potatoes, and she couldn't concentrate on finding on-line stores that carried placemats, bud vases, and the equipment. Emily took care of the big stuff while Sydney handled some of the minor details, the kitchen and menu. She needed to get a grip on her emotions and compartmentalize her thoughts, or she'd be a basket case.

Things had changed last night. Sydney felt the shift and sensed Jack did, too.

Footsteps echoed against the tile floor as Molly dragged her across the room and up the stairs into the dingy attic. When the girl pulled the string attached to the bare overhead bulb, the light pushed the gray back into the corners. Sydney searched the space, unsure where to start. Boxes, storage bins, and what looked like old furniture covered with sheets filled every inch of the room that ran the entire length of the depot. Dust captured in the shafts of light streaming through the dirt-encrusted windows floated in the air. She sneezed.

"Wow. Hoarder central." Emily bit her lip. "We only have a few hours, not weeks."

"True. I wonder what we'll find." Sydney widened her eyes as she glanced around the attic again.

Jack's heavy tread sounded on the stairs. "Who knows? Some of the stuff was here when my grandparents bought the place." In a moment, he placed his hands on his daughter's shoulders. "Some of it is stuff my grandparents and parents stored, and a few boxes are mine."

Molly widened her eyes. "There's stuff from Great *Oma* and *Opa*? I bet we'll find a treasure."

"I'm sure you will." He ruffled Molly's hair. "Let's see what we can use for the show."

"You never know what you'll discover." Sydney walked over to a stained sheet and lifted the corner. "Like this." With a flick of her wrist, she pulled off the fabric, revealing an old bench similar to the ones she'd seen on the depot porch in the museum picture. A cloud of dust rose and tickled the inside of her nose. Her sneeze filled the cramped area.

"Bless you." Emily, Jack, and Molly spoke at the same time.

"Thanks." She turned. "Emily, how about we put this bench downstairs along the far wall and add a few pillows for decoration or set it on the porch where people can sit while waiting for a table."

"That's a neat idea, Ms. Sydney. Can I help you decide where it should go?" Molly asked.

"Of course. Who better than the future owner?" Jack knelt by Molly and tweaked her nose.

Sydney had no argument there.

"Thanks, Daddy." Molly hugged her father.

At the bonding moment, happiness filled Sydney. For the brief time she was here, she'd make sure Jack and Molly had plenty more opportunities. "Let's hope we find more things we can repurpose and use downstairs."

****

A few minutes later, Jack wedged a hand through his hair again. The task unnerved him. The sun shifted again, pulling more light from the room. It could take days to go through everything, and what would he do with the stuff he no longer wished to keep?

He snapped off a well-worn, dusty sheet and held back a sneeze. "Let's put this bench downstairs, too, and free up more space. Do you think you can handle the weight, Sydney?"

"Of course. I bet the bench is more bulky than heavy. Another coat of stain on the wood, and spray paint on the wrought iron, and this thing will look brand new." She stepped forward and placed her hands on the wood seat. Her smile lit up the dim space, and his heart skipped a beat. Why did this woman cause such a reaction? Marin was the only one for him, but his heart refused to agree.

Redirecting his thoughts back to business, he thought of Sydney's earlier point. This bench could handle overflow patrons and would add a spark of interest to the barren porch. If he remembered the picture from the museum, other benches remained, too. One would fit well along the far wall by the fireplace.

"Ready. One. Two. Three." Jack spoke before he and Sydney lifted the bench in unison as if they'd done that action a hundred times before. Working together with her proved easy. More sweat broke out on his forehead. He should plan on how to speed up production, and not create reasons why he should delay things so she would stay. "We'll put it back on the porch for now. Molly, can you open the front door? I'll go down first."

Once Jack and Sydney relocated the other three benches outside, he glanced around the attic. They had created space, but the stacks of remaining boxes daunted him. Even with the designer's help, the group had their work cut out for them. "Emily, the Christmas stuff is on the right. We'll start on the other side. I'll take the left, Molly, you take the middle, and Sydney, you take the right. Open the boxes and see what's inside them first." Jack pulled two markers out of his pocket and handed one to Sydney and the other to his daughter. "Write the description on the side. I'll dispose of the junk. Anything useful can go downstairs."

"Jack, this area would make a great office." Sydney dusted her hands against her jeans. "If you cordoned off storage space and moved your desk and accessories here, you could convert the downstairs space into more dining or a room for private functions."

"That's a terrific idea, Ms. Sydney. Daddy, we can have birthday parties and tea parties like Mrs. Langley does at the Grand Hotel and host Christmas parties." Molly clapped and jumped up and down.

"I'll keep that in mind." Jack placated his daughter. Sydney's idea had merit. Too bad she wouldn't be here if he converted the spaces. The thought saddened him because over the past few days, her presence had grown on him. He'd screwed up things by kissing her last night. He wanted to hold her and press her soft lips against his every minute she was close, which was why he needed to stay clear.

Sydney Ryan represented a heartache, and he'd already had enough loss in his lifetime.

"Hey, look at these papers."

The woman of his thoughts broke the stillness, and Jack turned in time to see her pull a stack of old papers from her box.

"What are they, Ms. Sydney?" Molly dropped an old book she'd been reading. The thud echoed in the cramped area and caused a cloud of dust to rise as she skipped to Sydney's side.

"Old train schedules." She thumbed through the yellowed paper. "And not just the ones for the Silver Ridge Line, but the Denver lines, too."

"Those schedules were for passengers to know what time their trains left once they arrived in Denver." He approached and peered over her shoulder. "My dad told me about these, but I've never seen them. I always assumed he threw them away."

"I'm glad he didn't. From the looks of things, he didn't get rid of much." Sydney gazed at the papers in her hands.

"My mom told me Oma was a packrat. The mess drove my grandfather crazy. That's why the junk is here and not in a landfill." He'd already approved of the old steamer trunk and a few suitcases from the nineteen twenties Emily had discovered and planned on using as decorations downstairs.

Molly ran a finger along the timeline. "Only two trains left the station, Daddy?"

Jack nodded. "Silver Ridge was smaller back then, honey, and with more people owning cars, the need for rail travel dwindled. Keeping them running got too costly, so stations closed and lines merged or shut all together. The last train here ran on September tenth, 1960. My grandparents bought the building a few years later."

Molly's eyes grew wide. "Wow. If it hadn't closed, then Great *Oma* and *Opa* wouldn't have bought this place and we wouldn't own it now."

"That's right, honey." Jack fought to hide the dual emotion in his voice. He loved the restaurant because of the family legacy, but without Marin the ownership drained him at the same time. Sydney's reason for being here was to make Joe's Café successful again and free his time to spend with his daughter. Would the renovation work? Was the answer that simple?

"I love the drawing of the old train at the top and the large flowery lettering of the town along the side. Is that advertising?" Sydney pointed to the box with a more elegant font and a small, hand-drawn picture of the hotel front. "Rooms were fifteen dollars?"

"Apparently. I bet Larry and Cynthia would like a few copies. Larry's great-grandparents built the hotel, and I'm sure they'd like the memorabilia."

"I know they would. Cynthia told me all about the history." Sydney waved over her designer. "Emily, can we use these downstairs?"

Emily quit rummaging through a box, stood, and walked to Sydney. A smile filled the designer's face as she stared at the paper. "These schedules are fabulous. I'll order glass tops for the existing tables and place them underneath. The old paper and the well-worn, scarred surfaces will create the homey, nostalgic atmosphere without using tablecloths or placemats."

Jack covered his anger at the intentional slight and glanced at his cell phone. "That might work, but I want to approve the concept first. Ten minutes to five. A few more minutes and then we'll call it a night."

"Works for me." Sydney arched her back.

She smiled as if she'd gained a victory. Not yet. If he agreed, using the old train schedules satisfied her need for change and his desire to keep certain things the same, but he wouldn't be railroaded into something he couldn't see first. Unsure of what she'd uncover next, he strode over and knelt beside the box as Sydney set aside the train schedules. He pulled out another stack, revealing a faded color photo of the depot's exterior.

"Wow." Sydney gasped. "The photo is from 1957."

As she retrieved what appeared to be a stack of old

photos, a delighted smile filled her expression, and light danced in her eyes. If only he could get as excited. Finding the picture meant he could duplicate the exact colors if he chose to paint the outside come spring, but painting the place would change the depot's appearance and all the memories from his youth.

"It still looks the same. Kind of," Molly exclaimed.

"Now we know the exterior colors. If we're lucky, we'll find interior shots. Here. I'll let you do the honors." Sydney stepped closer and held out the stack of photos.

Her floral scent distracted him from the pieces of history in his hands. The weight of keeping Joe's Café open clung to his shoulders as he leafed through the stack. Finding them was a godsend and a curse because the colors complemented the exterior better than the palette his grandparents used.

If he followed Sydney's vision, nothing would remain of the place his grandparents established and where he proposed to Marin. Losing that connection to his late wife would feel like reliving her death all over again. But if he halted the production, Sydney would leave and create another hole in his vulnerable heart.

Chapter Eleven

"Hey, look. What's this?" Molly's question caught Sydney's attention.

In the dim light, she saw the girl pull out an old pair of brown breeches with straps. Embroidery complemented the front pockets and the piece of leather holding the two straps together.

"Oh my, what is that thing?" Emily laughed.

"*Lederhosen*. They must have belonged to my grandfather." Jack closed his box.

Sydney watched him scribble *old dishes* on the top. She'd peek later and decide if she could use them downstairs.

"Can I keep them?" Molly pulled them on over her jeans and blue sweater.

Jack's expression softened, and a tiny smile played on his lips. "Sure. Your Great *Oma's dirndl* dress should be in there, too. My *Oma* and *Opa* wore them when they met at a German festival back in the forties."

"You're right. Your grandmother didn't get rid of anything. How sweet she kept those outfits." Sydney sat on her heels and realized she'd never had anyone in her life to compare Jack's grandparents to. Sadness tugged at her heart, but she wasn't jealous. Maybe some day she'd have a similar type of family experience. "Your grandparents sound like special people."

"They were. Coming here after the war and starting

a business wasn't easy, but they did and passed the restaurant to my parents, who passed it to me." Jack fidgeted with his pen.

His uncertainty evident, Sydney wanted to reassure him. "And you'll pass Joe's Café to Molly." She stood and stretched. Going through the boxes was tedious and backbreaking, but they'd found the color photos. Who knew what else Jack would find when he got through everything?

"Look at me. I'm Kurt." Molly lifted her knees and moved her arms as she took a quick step forward and then back.

Sydney smiled and pushed a strand of hair behind her ear. Molly even wore the same expression the actor who played Kurt von Trapp in Sydney's favorite childhood movie.

Molly skipped and tugged on her father's arm. "Hey, Daddy. I'm dressed for the part, can we watch *The Sound of Music* tonight?"

Catching Jack's gaze, she smiled. He grinned back, and from the laugh lines at the corners of his eyes, she knew he remembered their conversation at the museum. Maybe next year before her new contract started, she'd make it to Austria, find a *dirndl* dress, and sing as she twirled through a meadow. If no one was listening, except Jack and Molly, suddenly, she didn't want to be there alone.

Jack broke the lingering eye contact and turned to his daughter. "Yes, you are, but the movie is long, sweetheart, and tomorrow will be busy."

She wanted to shake sense into the man. He acted like Georg von Trapp. She was surprised he didn't have a whistle, although if he did, she'd break it in two. His daughter needed his attention, and he was missing the perfect opportunity.

Molly sat on a box and folded her arms. "We haven't watched it in forever."

"Two months isn't forever, Molly." Jack grumbled.

"If you need me to cook tomorrow so Molly can sleep in, that won't be a problem. I'll try a few more specials and see how your customers respond." Sydney scheduled a meeting with the rest of the crew in the morning to discuss a few things, but with coaching, Emily could handle the job.

"Unnecessary, *Ms. Ryan*." Jack turned his back. "If we leave in the next few minutes, Molly, we'll order in a pizza, watch the movie, and you can still get to sleep at your normal bedtime."

She stuck out her bottom lip. "I want Ms. Sydney to join us, too."

Sydney's heart sank. She didn't want to intrude on Jack's time, and the more time she spent with the handsome restaurant owner and his daughter, the harder leaving would be when the time came.

****

At Emily's insistence, a few minutes before six, Sydney rang the doorbell of the two-story, red-brick bungalow with the white trim. She glanced around the uninviting porch running the length of the house. Dead leaves littered the wood planks, and snow lay piled in the corners. Like the depot, she imagined the house with a swing, a few potted flowers, and a welcome sign. Jack let the place go, too, because life overwhelmed him. Her heart again ached for Jack and Molly. She heard the deadbolt unlatch and the green wood door swung open, revealing Molly with a beaming face and wearing the *lederhosen* over her princess pajamas.

"Ms. Sydney, you came."

"I did. I wouldn't turn down dinner, a movie, and hanging out with my favorite girl for anything."

"Come in." Molly pulled her into the warm interior.

Sydney's smile froze when she caught sight of Jack descending the stairs, fresh from a shower, and his hair still damp.

He stopped and stood behind Molly.

She took in his clean scent and shaven face and bit her tongue. The man had no right to be so handsome and smell good. His gray sweatpants and white T-shirt only heightened her awareness.

Over-dressed in black slacks and a pink button-down shirt, Sydney groaned silently as heat burned her cheeks. Unlike her, he'd dressed for a comfortable evening watching a movie with his daughter.

Molly tugged her arm again and pulled her farther into the living room. "This way. The pizza will be here soon, and everything is ready. I made microwave popcorn and got the glasses for the pop." She pointed to the three cups filled with ice, the two-liter green bottle of amber liquid, and the bowl of popcorn on the rustic, wooden coffee table. "Soda's a treat, not a right, and I only get to drink it on special occasions, so thanks for coming over tonight," Molly whispered.

"You're welcome." Sydney glanced in Jack's direction and swallowed. So, despite his casual attire, he treated this evening as a special occasion. Her heart beat faster as she settled on the worn, overstuffed, beige-and-brown-striped couch. A roaring fire occupied the brick fireplace, adding a well-lived-in and cozy atmosphere. Two stockings hung from the wood mantle, and a tall Christmas tree dominated the corner. A photo of a smiling woman with long, dark hair and brown eyes hung above the fireplace—Molly's mother, Marin. Her daughter looked just like her. Sydney forced away her sadness. This was Molly's night.

The girl plopped next to Sydney while Jack poured the soda.

When their fingers connected as he handed her the glass, awareness affected her emotions. The room shifted, as if caught off axis, as she stared into his blue eyes. What a terrible idea. "Thanks." She broke the spell and glanced at Molly. "I can't wait to see this movie again. I haven't seen it in years."

"What's your favorite part?" Molly scooped up a handful of popcorn.

"Maria singing in the Alps. What's yours?" Sydney glanced at Jack and grinned. Mistake. She glanced at Molly.

"I like when the kids pull those pranks on Maria. And when she sings, and when she makes the curtains into their clothes, and when the Sisters tell Reverend Mother they have sinned to protect them. I guess I like everything." Molly giggled and ate her handful of popcorn.

"Hey, save room for the pizza." Jack settled on the other side of Molly and kicked off his slippers. He grabbed the remote and pushed the Play button.

Moments later, the movie filled the screen.

"The von Trapp children lost their mother, too. I like Maria. She's nice, like you, Ms. Sydney." Molly leaned in and linked their arms.

That's why Sydney liked the movie so much and

suspected Molly did, too. They both related to the motherless children. She heard Jack shift. Unable to pry her arm from Molly's grasp, Sydney quit trying and relished the warm and contented feeling that would remain long after the waning moon dipped below the horizon. Not only was Sydney starting to care for Jack, but she had also fallen for his daughter.

Three-and-a-half hours later, the movie credits rolled, and Jack shut off the TV. "Okay, Molly. Time for bed."

"Can Miss Sydney tuck me in? Please?" Molly tugged Sydney's hand.

Sydney removed the cups and the empty popcorn bowl from the table, and then wedged the bowl against her hip. Using her free hand, she grabbed the soda bottle and wrestled with her thoughts. She didn't want to intrude in their nightly routine or make Molly sad either. "Honey, that's your dad's place, but I'll say goodnight if your father agrees."

"Fine." Jack shrugged.

Sensing his disappointment, Sydney took her time putting the remaining soda in the refrigerator and finding room in the dishwasher for their glasses and pizza plates. Then she washed the popcorn bowl and placed it in the dish rack, feeling disconcerted, and like an intruder in Jack's home. Everywhere she looked, from the curtains, to the candles, to the cross-stitched *Bless This House* hanging in the foyer, she saw his late wife's presence. If she hadn't promised to tuck in Molly, she would have escaped into the chilly night.

Five minutes later, Jack held out her coat before he shrugged into his. "I'll walk you to your car."

"You don't have to."

"I do." Jack opened the front door and ushered her outside. "You drove over here because I couldn't leave the fire unattended."

"You don't have to explain yourself. I didn't mind the brief drive." Sydney picked her way, avoiding patches of ice in his driveway. His firm grip on her elbow assured she wouldn't slip. She unlocked the doors and waited for him to release her. Instead, he turned her to face him. Butterflies whirled in her stomach, and her breath caught in her throat at his tender expression.

"Thanks for spending the evening with us. Molly had a great time. I did to."

His warm breath fanned her cheek. A low growl escaped before his head dipped and his lips claimed hers again, the action chasing away the night's chill. Sydney responded by wrapping her arms around his neck, pulling him closer. The longer she kissed him, the deeper she fell in love. *Love.* The absurd idea rattled in her brain. She'd never experienced this feeling. Deepening the kiss, she never wanted the night to end, until she realized the cold, stark reality of her life was in L.A. and his was here.

"I have to leave. Good night, Jack. See you tomorrow." Before she did something stupid and declared her love, she escaped his grasp.

****

"Come on, Ms. Sydney. Let's go." Molly tugged Sydney's gloved hand.

Jack's daughter pointed at the ice-skating rink late Sunday afternoon. With skepticism, Sydney stared at the makeshift rink at the resort on the outskirts of town. She glanced at Jack, who stood on the other side of his daughter. Tiny laugh lines crinkled around his eyes, making the heat rise in her cheeks. He must have remembered her comment about the rental car.

"Can I sit this one out?" She didn't want to leave the warmth of the fire in the fire pit. The benches lining the rink where other people sat watching the gaggle of skaters looked more promising and safer. Sydney and ice did not mix. The last time she'd tried at the make-shift rink in Santa Monica, she'd had a lot of intimate contact between the ice and her jean-clad rear-end. Her falling was all Martin and Ricardo needed to catch on film for a pickup shot. Her feet wobbled while on solid ground.

Molly pulled again. "If I can do it, you can, too. Come on, it will be fun."

For who? Sydney, or all the people who would realize the reality TV star couldn't skate if her life depended on it. She should have taped bubble wrap to her bottom so she wouldn't bruise anything more than her ego.

Skating wasn't Sydney's idea of a fun, but Emily insisted. What better way to get the flavor of the town than by having Sydney take part in all the activities? Was her designer playing matchmaker? Emily's recent engagement made her think every single woman in the world should have a ring, too. Sydney's life was fine. She peeked at Jack and thought about last night.

Or was it?

Unlike other projects where she anticipated the end of production, she wanted to draw out this one for weeks. She liked Silver Ridge. The Caymans didn't seem as exotic as roasting marshmallows and eating s'mores by the fire with Jack and Molly. She shook her head. What was she thinking? She'd earned, and needed, her vacation after this unexpected production that required a quick turnaround. Sydney had too much to do before filming started, but another glance at Jack made her forget everything.

"Would you prefer if I hold your arm?" Jack whispered.

"I'd appreciate that." More heat burned her cheeks. She didn't want to disappoint the girl who wormed her way into Sydney's heart, and with Jack's help, she wouldn't humiliate herself in front of her national or local audience. Sydney wasn't a quitter. Each time she'd experienced a setback before, she'd risen to the challenge, like she would here.

"It'll be fun. I promise." He cupped her elbow.

Jack's crooked grin set her heartbeat on overdrive as he maneuvered her into the rink. The smooth ice took her off-guard, and she floundered before gathering her balance. Jack's presence helped steady her, because breaking an arm or a leg would not help with the time-sensitive production schedule. She inhaled, taking in his cologne along with the cool crisp air tinged with pine and smoke.

"You're doing great, Ms. Sydney. Just don't look down." Molly grinned.

Determination filled Sydney. If Molly or the toddler who zoomed past could do it, she could, too. Of course, Molly's center of gravity was lower, and she was closer to the ice if she fell.

"We'll stick to the edge. Lean forward a little. It'll help with your balance." Jack coached.

Sydney liked the way his protective grip tightened; something she'd never experienced. She'd always fended for herself and found letting another person lead strange and exhilarating. After watching another skater glide by, her confidence faltered. The woman in purple made remaining upright look so easy.

"Just pretend you're marching, Ms. Sydney." Molly took a few steps and skated across the ice.

"Seems simple enough." Sydney smiled and mimicked her actions, thrilled she glided forward while maintaining her balance. With luck, she'd be a pro at the end of the century if she kept practicing.

"That's great." Molly beamed and gave her a thumbs-up.

"Keep doing that and you won't need my help anymore," Jack whispered in her ear.

"Doubtful." The breath squeezed from Sydney's lungs. Jack's nearness did crazy things. She needed to concentrate on staying upright instead of recognizing how right his touch felt.

"Let's go to the center. I'll show you how to stop and how to swizzle."

Jack urged her forward. "Swizzle?" Surprised, Sydney didn't fall as Jack led her into the middle. She'd gotten more used to the ice, but she was not as comfortable as the other skaters. Jack released her. When she was free from his grip, she felt adrift until he faced her and grabbed her arms.

"Hold on."

Sydney grasped his forearms. The skaters, the camera, and the world disappeared as she stared into the depths of his eyes that matched the color of the darkening sky. She could fall into them and never leave. She remembered his caresses. Splash.

Jack skated backward and dragged Sydney along.

"Now, put your heels together and force them outward. Then point your toes inward. That move is called a swizzle. You're creating an hourglass shape on the ice. This move will get you used to the skating sensation."

Yanking her thoughts from Jack's kiss and concentrating on the task, Sydney followed Jack's instruction and glided over the smooth ice. She grinned. "I'm skating!"

Molly clapped. "I knew you could do it, Ms. Sydney. Daddy, a group of kids from my class is over there. Can I skate with them?"

Jack nodded. "Be careful, and don't leave the rink unless you tell me."

"I won't." In a flash Molly skated away.

"I wonder if I'll ever skate well." As Sydney continued to weave her skates in and out, her confidence grew.

"I don't see why not? It takes practice. I'm sure each remodel got easier. Skating is the same way. Let's practice a few more minutes, and then we'll get a cup of hot chocolate and warm up by the fire."

"Works for me." Sydney sighed in relief. Even though she'd gotten better, firm ground under her feet would be a welcome change.

"Hi, Jack," a female voice called.

Sydney turned to watch the stylish, early-thirtysomething brunette with the chin-length hair skate over and stop with an ease Sydney could never pull off. She wanted to brush the ice shavings from her skates, but Sydney had no wish to humiliate herself by falling over. Restaurant renovations and Chef Bruno she handled with no problem. Two pieces of metal strapped onto her feet while standing on ice left a lot to be desired even with Jack's instruction.

"Nadine." Jack's lips pressed into a firm line.

He tightened his grip on her arms. Sydney wanted to escape from the woman who had her white ski jacket unzipped at the top, revealing a low-cut, tight-fitting sweater. The blue angora accentuated a certain part of her anatomy Sydney lacked. Unable to break free, she struggled to remain upright while other skaters zipped by. The possessive way the woman spoke Jack's name, and her apparent familiarity, sent unease spiraling through Sydney.

"Where's Ethan?" Jack looked away.

"He's off with other kids in his class, and I'm all by my lonesome." She batted her eyelashes.

The woman pouted. Her charm didn't affect Jack, but a few other men in the rink almost bumped into each other, paying more attention to the brunette than their skating. The cloying scent the woman poured on wafted under Sydney's nose. She held back a sneeze.

"I believe Molly is one of them." Jack waved toward where a group of children huddled in the corner. "Have you met Sydney Ryan?" Jack leaned close.

His warmth created havoc. Soon she'd have to identify these feelings, but not until she was safe on non-slippery ground.

"No, I haven't. I heard a ruckus about a minor celebrity here to slap on paint and degrease the menu at the diner. Hi, Ms. Ryan. I'm Nadine Boyd. I'm sure Jack's mentioned me?" Nadine arched a shaped eyebrow and tapped red manicured nails against her jacket.

"I can't say he has. Hi, Nadine." When the woman didn't accept her handshake, Sydney dropped her hand

and stiffened at the intentional slight.

"Sydney and I are leaving to drink hot chocolate. Now if you'll excuse us..." Jack announced.

Underneath his silky words, Sydney sensed his continued agitation. She watched him search for an opening to get her to the edge of the rink, only too glad to leave the other woman's unwanted company.

"Hot chocolate sounds divine. Thank you, Jack." Nadine purred.

Sydney sighed. The woman wasn't so easy to shake as she watched her glide effortlessly across the ice and seductively sway of her hips.

Back on solid ground, Sydney's relief was temporary as she and Jack walked toward the closest firepit. The afternoon started with so much promise and ended in disaster. At least Sydney hadn't humiliated herself by falling on the ice, but she'd made an enemy.

"I'll be right back." Jack settled her on the only empty bench in the area.

After what looked like an uneasy glance at Nadine, he hesitated before he released Sydney's arm and strode to the table filled with a big urn and rows of white, take-out coffee cups.

Nadine settled next to her.

She inched away, almost falling off the bench. When Jack returned, he'd have to wedge in next to Molly's classmate's mother, unless he chose to stand.

"Just so you know, Jack and I are an item. Don't get any ideas," Nadine hissed.

The woman's voice was low enough for only Sydney to hear. *Ouch.* Nadine got straight to the point. She'd fit with a certain set in L.A. Sydney sat straighter, squared her shoulders, and faced the woman.

The other woman had curves, but still Sydney had height. "Jack is a big boy and can make his own decisions, but don't worry. I'm here to fix his place, nothing more."

She had no designs on Jack, even though Sydney still hadn't recovered from their kiss last night. Heat scorched her cheeks again. Something wasn't right. Either the woman lied about her relationship with Jack, or the man was a cad. Her stomach clenched, and bile hit the back of her throat. Sydney ought to give him a piece of her mind.

"Keep it that way." Nadine unzipped her jacket.

As the woman further accentuated her abundant curves, Sydney heard the venom and understood the message.

"Here you go, Sydney." Jack held out a cup. "Nadine?" He handed a second one to the other woman.

Nadine eyed him like he was the cup of freshly made hot chocolate. The woman's predatory action sickened her.

"Thank you." Nadine cooed, put down the cup, stood, and then wrapped her arms around his neck. "So nice of you to think of me, Jack. I'm fundraising with the PTO again. We hope you'll donate another gift certificate for the silent auction at the winter carnival. Let's talk about it over a cup of coffee at my place tomorrow."

Before she kissed Jack, Nadine glanced at her through squinted eyelids.

Anger curled around her heart. Sydney had seen enough. The man had a lot of nerve, and to think she'd fallen for his charm. She fought the urge to touch her lips and brush away the memory of his caress. "Thanks for a delightful afternoon, Jack." Sydney stood. "Please say goodbye to Molly for me. See you in the morning."

With as much dignity as she could muster with skates strapped to her feet, Sydney wobbled toward the parking lot. As she waved to Martin and Ricardo, she realized the cameraman captured the entire interaction. She plastered on a smile and slashed her hand across her throat. How many more times would Jack humiliate her in front of her crew?

Chapter Twelve

"Sydney—wait." Disgusted, Jack pulled Nadine's arms from his neck and stepped back.

Too late. The reality star was surrounded by her crew and a few adoring fans, reminding him Sydney came from a different world. Once she returned to hers, Jack would remain in Silver Ridge and deal with the nonstop gossip that went along with living in a small community.

He stared at Nadine, who'd expressed her interest for two years, but she'd never been aggressive. Why now? She sensed a competition with Sydney Ryan that didn't exist, because dating didn't interest Jack. If it did, the woman wouldn't be Sydney, although kissing her rocked him to the core.

After this escapade, if he did, Nadine was out of the question, too.

Jack rubbed the back of his neck. He wanted to sprint after Sydney, but he needed to set this woman straight before Molly returned. "What was that nonsense, Nadine?"

"I don't know what you're talking about." The woman adjusted her jacket, tucked her hair behind her ear, and smiled. "You know me well, don't you, Jack? Since fourth grade. Our kids are the same age, and you need to move on with your life, for Molly's sake."

Jack ignored all her subtle and not-so-subtle hints.

No one would tell him when to date. He didn't know if his heart could get involved with another woman again and face the possibility that she might die, too. "I'll decide when I'm ready, Nadine. As for another gift certificate? No problem. I'll send it to school with Molly before winter break. Now if you'll excuse me…" He turned on his heel to go after Sydney, but she'd disappeared in the crowd.

Clenching his hands, he sank onto the nearest bench and rested his back against the cold seeping through the cracks in the old wood. Why had he ever kissed her? That action had been reckless and stupid. So why did he want to drive over to the hotel, pull her close, and relive the kiss he dreamed about all day and night?

He'd fallen hard for Sydney Ryan.

****

"Quiet, please. Are we ready?" Philip Townsend boomed from his perch on the bar stool Monday morning as he flipped through his notebook.

Jack eyed the fortysomething director sporting round glasses, a long, blond ponytail, and a diamond stud earring Sydney introduced yesterday.

"And action." Philip pointed toward Sydney.

As she closed the café's front door, Sydney smiled and stared into the camera. She walked into the restaurant's interior.

His heart raced.

"Hi, and welcome to another episode of *Ryan to the Rescue*. Today I'm at Joe's Café in Silver Ridge, Colorado. A few weeks ago, the studio received a letter from Mary-Katerina Quinn, asking us to help her father, so here we are."

"Cut," Philip shouted and scribbled a few notes on the paper attached to his clipboard. "Again, from the top. Walk slower, Sydney. Martin, move to the right for a different angle."

Jack watched the filming from the safety of his office doorway. He rubbed a hand across his face. Production had begun, and now nothing would stop it. He had to allow Sydney to make over his place, or let Joe's Café die a slow, painful death. Which was worse?

"I can't believe the number of people and how much equipment it takes." Uncle Ray shifted and whistled.

"I know. The restaurant seems small," Mrs. Collins whispered back. "There're no customers today. What will it be like during the Grand Opening when the tables are full?"

"Not sure how everyone will fit." Uncle Ray agreed. "Glad I'm in the kitchen."

"I'm ecstatic Cynthia is sending two of her girls to help. I'm not sure I could keep up." Mrs. Collins shook her head.

"You'll do fine, my dear." Uncle Ray grinned.

"Quiet again."

The director spoke with authority, quieting Jack's employees. Glad for the silence, Jack watched the pre-filming sequence again. His employees' banter got on his nerves. He should be in the office placing orders and paying bills, not staring at Sydney, but he couldn't help himself.

She hadn't spoken to him all morning outside of a hello when she and her crew arrived. She obviously avoided him because of Nadine's blatant attempt in pretending a relationship existed. Jack had never asked out Nadine or even suggested the possibility. She was just another mother of one of Molly's classmates. Her kiss left him feeling like he'd puckered up with a dead fish as opposed to Sydney's warm and passionate caress.

Jack was in trouble.

Mrs. Collins would be pleased.

Even though she'd never spoken about the subject, her direct hints by mentioning every eligible woman in Silver Ridge hadn't gone unnoticed. She wanted him to remarry. Not an easy feat when he didn't date. Thankfully, she wasn't at the skating rink Sunday afternoon, so she didn't witness the debacle with Nadine.

He wasn't happy about the Nadine situation. Soon, he would broach the subject with Sydney if she ever uttered another word to him again outside of production. He missed their conversations, and it had only been a few hours.

As he watched Sydney, Jack thought about her nestling in his arms and her lips molding to his during their brief kisses. She filled the void in his life and made him realize what he missed.

"She looks like she does on TV," Mrs. Collins spoke in a hushed voice once the director called cut.

"Hard to believe she's here," Uncle Ray whispered back. "You made the right choice, son."

Did he? Jack glanced at the mess inside Joe's Café and squeezed the bridge of his nose. Since Sydney blew in with that blizzard ten days ago, both his restaurant and his life descended into chaos. He saw nothing changing until filming was complete and she returned to L.A.

When she left, he and Molly would experience the pain of another loss.

****

Jack watched Sydney Tuesday morning as she took a sip of coffee. He never thought about all the behind-the-scenes work. Days' worth of filming would be compressed into an hour episode minus the commercials. If he was exhausted, he knew she had to be, too. The crew arrived at 4:00 am today, and he suspected Sydney was the one who let them inside Joe's Café.

He didn't know because she'd avoided him all day yesterday. She wasn't so lucky today with the interior clips with him in the front and back of the house. Everything depended on how much they accomplished before Molly returned from school. Sydney had been true to her word and kept the production away from his daughter.

A position he wished for. Still uncomfortable with the cameras and microphone, he couldn't wait until this nightmare ended. All the attention ate at his composure. At her request, he joined her at the table.

"Okay, Jack. Try to relax." She placed a hand on his arm.

He wasn't surprised at the surge of energy. Sydney had that effect, and he'd miss it once she departed. That thought saddened him. He'd grown accustomed to her presence in his café and his life. "Easier said than done."

"All I'll do in this next scene is introduce you and ask the questions Zach provided you yesterday."

Jack clenched his fists together. All business, but what had he expected? "How much time do we have?"

"Ten minutes."

Her smile should reassure him, but it didn't. While her lips might have curved upwards, her eyes remained lifeless, and he suspected her reaction was all his fault. He'd wanted to talk yesterday, but she'd evaded him. "About Sunday…"

She shook her head. "Not my business, so no explanation necessary."

"One is necessary." Jack flexed a hand, focusing his attention anywhere but the woman who sat kitty-corner. "Nadine is one of Molly's classmate's mothers. I've known her for years. Long before we had kids. Since I was in fourth grade to be exact. She was soliciting a donation, that's all."

"A donation?" Sydney's eyebrows rose.

He detected her sarcasm. She didn't believe him. Why should she? Nadine's actions suggested they were an item, and especially her nauseating kiss. He swallowed. "Yes." Jack fought the urge to stand and pull Sydney into his arms. All this talk about kissing made him edgy, and he wanted to touch her lips again. "I donate a twenty-five-dollar gift certificate for the café every year to the school's winter fundraiser."

"How generous. I'm sure the school appreciates your donation. Nadine, too. Now if you'd like to run through the questions—"

"Sydney—" Jack stopped her when she tried to stand. Despite her long sleeve T-shirt, the heat of her skin scorched him. The elegant slope of her neck invited his gaze to linger, and the delicate scent of berries drifted under his nose. He almost forgot why she was here. "Nothing exists between Nadine and me. I've never dated her or given her any sign of interest. And after Sunday's stunt, if I do date again, the woman won't be her."

Feeling her resistance, he tightened his grip.

"Who you date is your choice as it is mine. The same for kisses."

"I didn't want to kiss Nadine." He passed his free hand across his face before rubbing his eyes. The woman was not making this conversation easy, but then again everything had become complicated the minute she'd walked through the front door. He lost himself in the depths of her expressive eyes. Why did all reason and judgment disappear near her? All he thought about was her lips, her passion, her love for what she did, and for his restaurant. He wanted to capture that passion again. "I wanted to kiss you, Sydney. I still do."

This time, Sydney freed herself and stood.

"That kiss meant nothing, Jack. It happened at the spur of the moment and shouldn't have. We were both vulnerable and unsure, and given the romance of the holiday season, something was bound to happen. Now if you'll excuse me, I have things to go over with Philip before we start."

Disappointed, Jack watched her go. She was right. The kiss meant nothing. So why did he want to steal another one before he embarrassed himself on national television and in front of her crew? Because she was wrong. Her kiss meant everything, and he suspected his meant a lot, too, or she wouldn't be avoiding him.

****

By early afternoon, Jack felt more comfortable as he stood behind the line. Or as comfortable as he could be with the wireless microphone attached under his shirt and two cameras ready to capture his every movement. The slew of people made his kitchen feel smaller, but at least he did something familiar, unlike the earlier segment where he talked to Sydney while the cameras rolled.

"Okay, so in this scene, Frank and Ray will prepare the orders coming into the kitchen. Sydney will observe. Jack, you'll be next to Sydney so she can communicate what she sees." Philip adjusted his glasses and studied the papers on his clipboard.

After being a part of the production this morning, Jack knew enough to wait until the pre-shooting sequence was over and the director called action.

Suddenly, Uncle Ray had two left thumbs. Frank and Uncle Ray always worked in tandem behind the line. Today the men bumped into each other, and their timing was off. So much in fact, Uncle Ray burnt a few pieces of toast and had to remake three eggs. Jack should have requested hired actors because this scene made his staff look incompetent. He should have never agreed to do the episode.

"One number three, two number ones, one scrambled with bacon, the other over easy with sausage," Uncle Ray snapped. "Where are you on the order for table nine? The french toast is done."

"Coming right up." Frank plated the omelet and potatoes.

With all the chaos and distraction in the kitchen, the cooks struggled to keep up.

"Where's the order for the Watsons on six? Max, can you refill the waters and coffees, please?" Brianne, the petite blonde teenager who stood in for Mrs. Collins, grabbed the two plates and hurried to the door.

Jack strode behind the line and scanned the tickets

hanging on the wheel. When he couldn't find the Watson's order, he sucked in a breath and his stomach nose-dived. All this confusion was being captured for Sydney's audience. "Where's the order for table six, Uncle Ray?"

"Went out five minutes ago." Uncle Ray wiped his forehead with a sleeve. He arched his back and slowly wiped his hands on the towel hung over the tie of his apron.

"Then why is Brianne asking about it?" Jack stared at his number two cook.

His uncle was slow when Jack needed him to be on his A game. Jack grabbed the spindle and ruffled through the slips of completed orders. Six slips down, he found the missing ticket. The order hadn't been cooked because he hadn't seen a Belgian waffle go out. "The order's right here. Are you okay, Uncle Ray?"

"That would explain why those two plates are still here." Uncle Ray nodded toward the two plates of scrambled eggs, bacon, and toast on the counter.

"Uncle Ray, why don't you get a cup of coffee, and I'll help Frank for a few minutes."

"Works for me." Uncle Ray again wiped his hands.

Jack swore he saw a fraction of a smile on his uncle's face as he stepped from behind the line. He shook his head at his imagination. His uncle wouldn't do anything to compromise the café. Taking charge, he reread the ticket. "A waffle with a side of hash browns and sausage. A number one scrambled with bacon and whole wheat. I'll start the waffle." A few minutes later, he saw Sydney yank the top plate from the stack.

"Stop. You can't serve food on here." She frowned and held out the plate.

The cameras rolled, and the sounds of the people breathing filled his ears. He'd forgotten about them until Sydney joined him behind the line. Instead of focusing on cooking, all he'd thought about was her fresh, berry scent and how he wanted to kiss her. Jack scratched the back of his neck. *Focus.* How had the well-used plate gotten back in the rotation? Sydney kicked his foot. He should have read the notes.

"What's wrong with it?" Even though they'd scripted this part, his unease increased in front of the cameras, and his lines didn't sound natural. Jack wiped his brow with the sleeve of his T-shirt.

"The plate's chipped."

He shrugged and turned his attention to plating the waffle. "Most of the plates are. The customers don't mind. Bacon please? You're delaying the order."

"Yes, I am." Sydney marched to the trash can and dumped the plate inside.

"Hey, that was a good plate," Jack grumbled.

She walked back and drilled her finger into his chest. "A roomful of paying customers who expect high quality from the food to the plate wait outside. Max, pull all the chipped plates and throw them in the dumpster."

"Yes, ma'am," the dishwasher and bus boy replied.

"Max. Put them on the far shelf." The scene gave him a sense of déjà-vu, except for the part where he grabbed her waist, pulled her close, and lost himself in her eyes. He stroked the softness of her skin before he leaned and grazed her heavenly lips.

****

What was Jack doing? Didn't he know he had an audience? Sydney should stop him and not keep responding to his touch. Why did she stand there instead of working on the order for table six?

Shouldn't Philip call cut?

Sydney should answer the questions, not enjoy the touch of Jack's fingertips on her cheek and his mouth on her lips. He made her feel special...cherished... loved. Something she wasn't used to but could be if given the chance.

The hinges on the kitchen door squeaked. "Is table six ready yet?" Briana questioned. "Oops."

Jack and Sydney broke apart.

Her breathing ragged, she fought for control as heat ravaged her cheeks. She shielded her face from the camera. "Oh, for Pete's sake, Martin. Cut." She adjusted her chef jacket to salvage what remained of the food and her dignity.

"This scene will be a great clip for this year's Christmas party." Martin, the camera man, laughed.

Sydney waved a spatula. "Philip, if this clip goes anywhere outside this kitchen, heads will roll, starting with yours."

****

Just before three that afternoon, Sydney and some of her crew sat at the table by the window. With Molly expected any moment, she'd kept her promise to Jack. Lauren, the assistant producer, wasn't happy, but she understood when Sydney reminded her about Jack's condition. She'd also reminded her not to film Molly, or Jack would call off the entire thing. So far, everyone did their job, and things were on schedule.

She glanced outside and saw Mr. and Mrs. White.

The two snowmen grinned back.

Before she returned to L.A., she'd have to take a

picture to remember the moment. Sadness grabbed her heart. She'd miss Silver Ridge and two of the occupants once she left. "Martin, can you get a pickup shot of the two snowmen?"

"Sure thing. Fits right in with all the other bonus interior and exterior clips." Martin laughed.

Cradling the white ceramic coffee cup, she took a sip. She wasn't thirsty, but she wanted to do something, or she'd touch her lips and remember Jack's caress. *Focus.* After a final glance, she eyed the construction foreman, knowing he was the right person to get this place completed on time. "So, let me get the timeline straight, Justin. You need two full days to complete the remodel?"

"Yes, if the guys and I start by four, we should be finished by mid-afternoon Friday. Can't do anything outside but change the light fixtures and refinish the benches."

"Becca told me. Don't focus on the exterior, but Emily, can you put up Christmas decorations to detract from the needed paint job?"

The decorator finished scribbling a note in her book and looked up. "Will do. Everything's ordered."

Things were coming together, but Sydney didn't want a job to end. She forced away her sadness. Her vacation, her next renovation, and her new contract would keep her mind focused on what she would miss. "Good. Will you have enough time to finish?"

Emily nodded. "I should. Everything's ready to go. New chairs and stools will be delivered Friday morning and everything else on Thursday. The worst-case scenario is everyone will have to pitch in at the midnight hour, so we can get it done."

"Not a problem. The new menu is ready, so we can do the big reveal to the employees Saturday morning." Pushing aside her personal feelings, she allowed her business persona to take over, and Sydney couldn't wait to see what her crew did to Jack's place. She had the concept, but at times she couldn't visualize the end result. She trusted Emily, and her designer had never failed to come through. Keeping the railroad theme would work wonders with updating the café from seventies to chic. She hoped Jack liked the remodel.

Lauren tapped her smart phone screen and placed it in her purse. "Then we'll do the grand opening and film the customer reactions. We'll do a few final pickup shots on Sunday, and then we'll be on a plane to California."

"We will." Tears stung Sydney's eyes, and a hollowness filled her heart. After Sunday, Silver Ridge would become a distant memory. She dreaded the end of production and wanted to linger in the Christmas atmosphere and at Joe's Café with Jack and Molly.

Five minutes later, the bell over the door jingled.

Molly popped in, a flurry of arms and legs as she skittered across the room. She dropped her backpack and gave Sydney a hug.

The girl's jacket still felt cold from the outside.

"Hi, Ms. Sydney. Hi, Daddy."

"Hi, Molly." Sydney caught a glimpse of Jack's pained expression. His daughter's words and actions hurt him again, and as before, he had every right to be upset. Molly should greet and hug her father first. Jack's daughter was growing attached, but the feeling was mutual. She extracted herself from Molly's hug.

"Where is everyone?" Molly glanced around.

"We're done for today, so the crew went to the hotel which is where I need to go." Sydney rubbed her forehead. Fatigue settled across her shoulders, and a headache pounded behind her right eye. If she didn't take a pain reliever and rest, a full-blown migraine would debilitate her. To dull the pain, she pressed a finger against her eyelid. "I have a few things to do, and the construction will start once your father is finished."

Molly's smile faded, and her lip quivered.

Sydney shouldn't have spent so much time with Jack's daughter, and her heart ached. She needed to distance herself. This was Jack's time. As the tension bit into her neck, the pain behind her eye increased. She needed space from the man oozing an appeal impossible to evade so she could clear her head of any residual emotions from his kiss. Her film crew would make hay with the footage. Months could pass before she lived that one down and before she forgot Jack and Molly Ransom of Silver Ridge, Colorado.

A dejected pout crossed the young girl's features.

Sadness consumed Sydney as she crouched and pushed a loose strand of hair behind Molly's ear. She'd miss Jack's daughter during the next few days and when she left. A sigh escaped. "I'm sorry, Molly. I'm busy the rest of the week."

****

"Everything okay?" Emily joined Sydney by the fireplace in the hotel that evening. "Here, you need a drink." She held out a glass.

"Thanks. I do, and everything's as fine as it can be." With a pensive smile, Sydney accepted the white wine the designer purchased in the restaurant. She'd taken a pain reliever upon returning, rested a few minutes, and got control over her headache. Her emotional state was another story.

Emily settled onto the overstuffed chair to her right.

A fire burned in the stone hearth, bathing the area in soft light. She basked in the warmth, sipped the crisp wine, and let the liquid settle on her tongue before she swallowed. Outside the large window, darkness descended, and the streetlights illuminated the wrought iron post wrapped in garland and lights and topped with a red bow. Piped-in Christmas carols competed with the crackling of the logs.

"Well, that sounds ominous. Anything I can do to help?" Emily swirled her wine.

"I'm not sure you can." Sydney took another sip. Solving her problems with alcohol never helped, but a glass tonight would ease her restlessness when she'd been in one place too long. She furrowed her brows. Or was there another reason?

She'd rather be with Jack and Molly, but common sense prevailed. The girl had become too attached, and to be honest, Sydney felt the same way. More time together would only complicate matters and make leaving harder, especially after today's kitchen incident. Now she wished she hadn't promised to attend the festival Saturday night.

"I'm a good listener."

"I know. I'm not sure you can help." Sydney's sigh filled the air, and she squeezed the glass as she stared at the presents under the Christmas tree, contemplating her empty life. Sure, she had her show, but that hadn't been very satisfying this past week. The odor of pine drifted under her nose. She'd never had a Christmas tree, and except for bringing back staff gifts from her vacation, she hadn't bought a present in years. How had her life become so complicated?

"Is it about what happened in the kitchen today?" Emily broke into her thoughts.

"You heard?" Sydney was glad Emily had the grace enough not to mention the kiss. Heat consumed her cheeks, and she stopped the urge to brush her fingers across her lips.

"Martin showed me all three beautiful minutes of the clip. I'm glad you let someone into your life."

"Despite how it appears, nothing is going on." So why did she feel dizzy and her heartbeat go crazy when they were together, and she got light-headed just thinking about him?

"Could have fooled me. That kiss was the real deal. The way he looked at you was…amazing…like nobody else existed."

Sydney ignored Emily's words. She didn't want to think about Jack, the kiss, or Molly, and how much she adored the child and her father. "Do Becca and Marv know?"

"I'm sure." Emily grinned and sipped her wine. "You usually don't get so involved. It's sweet and romantic. A single dad, an adorable child, snow, fires, and Christmas. Love is in the air."

"You read way too many romance novels." The season's magic overshadowed her time here. Nothing existed between them, except perhaps both were lonely.

Emily frowned. "I don't see anything wrong with romance books. Should I lend you a few? Spend your holidays here with someone you care about instead of another country. Quit hiding from your emotions."

Sydney paused. Being realistic wasn't hiding. "You sound like Becca. It doesn't matter. My life's in L.A., and their lives are here."

"If you don't explore what's happening, you're making a big mistake. You might not see, but everyone else does. Think about it." Emily raised her glass. "A toast. To Silver Ridge and Joe's Café, to Jack and Molly Ransom, and to finding happiness and love this Christmas."

She clicked her glass against Emily's. "I'll toast to a successful makeover and to Jack and Molly. I'm satisfied and don't need the complication of love."

"Nothing is wrong with love." Her designer protested.

As Sydney took another sip, a soft glow that had nothing to do with the fire radiated contentment. Emily's eyes sparkled. Was that what love looked like? She didn't have any experience in that department. "That's easy for you to say, Ms. Bride-to-be."

Her designer stared at her diamond ring. "Yep, and proud of it. I expect you to be in front when I throw my bouquet in June."

"Not me." Sydney wagged her finger and shook her head. "I'll be at the wedding, but I'm allergic to all things traditional and sentimental. Let someone who believes in all that stuff catch it."

Emily laughed and grinned. "I could be wrong, but I might be in the front row catching your bouquet first."

An image of Jack in a tux, standing at the altar, waiting for her to walk down the aisle rose in her mind's eye. Sydney blinked. Nonsense. She'd gone certifiably crazy.

Chapter Thirteen

"Okay, everyone. This is it." Sydney spoke to the assembled crowd.

Her voice surrounded Jack like a warm blanket. He hadn't seen her since Wednesday, but his reaction remained the same. As he stood on the café's front porch, he shivered, his breath dissipating in the still air.

The new coach lights pushed away the darkness and illuminated the faces of all his employees and two teenage girls borrowed from Larry and Cynthia. The garland-wrapped railing, posts, and doorway hid the faded and peeling paint, and a few red bows added a splash of color to the drab exterior. A wreath decorated with white lights, small red bows and old-fashioned kitchen Christmas tree ornaments hung from the front door, covering the window and blocking the interior from view.

Sydney's designer, Emily, had done a great job. He wouldn't have to wait much longer to see if he'd made a big mistake by letting the reality star renovate. He wished Molly could see it, but he'd sent her to spend the night with Sam to keep her off-camera.

"This scene is the big reveal. You all go in first. The cameras will catch everyone's expressions." Sydney squeezed his hand.

At her hesitant smile, he realized she was nervous, too. Why? He sucked air into his lungs and clenched his fists. What had she done to the place?

"Places, people," Philip called. "It's cold out here. Let's get everyone inside."

A few minutes later, Jack widened his eyes after he stepped through the doorway. Beside him, he heard everyone gasp.

"It's beautiful." Mrs. Collins, put her reaction into words first.

"Amazing. Simply amazing." His uncle whistled under his breath. "Never seen this place look so good."

"I hope the kitchen got updated, too." Frank sidestepped Jack and headed toward the new double doors.

Jack strode farther into the room and spun a three-sixty to take in everything.

"Well, what do you think?" Sydney questioned beside him.

Thrusting a hand through his hair, he surveyed the damage. Anger and despair warred inside. Sydney Ryan and her crew obliterated everything recognizable from Marin's, his parents', or grandparents' time. The only thing remaining was the repainted sign on the wall behind the counter. *When you're here, you're part of our family.* He spun on his heels. "What have you done to my restaurant?"

She stiffened.

Her eyes turned from the warmth of green summer grass to the cold, hard, greenish-blue glass pebbles filling the flower vases.

"I've made it into a chic, go-to destination that will draw in customers, and they'll linger." Sydney planted her fists on her hips.

"I operate on volume. This place is nothing like we

discussed." Jack hadn't felt this betrayed since his wife died.

Sydney crossed her arms. "Things changed, Mr. Ransom. We ran into a few problems, forcing us to make last-minute modifications. The changes are better than the initial plans."

Jack didn't agree. "What happened to the original paint scheme?"

"No one told me the store mixed up our order until the crew finished painting. I kept the new colors to adhere to the schedule. You can change them later if you wish."

He glanced around again. A bluish-green paint covered the wood paneling, while black with hints of dark brown highlighted the chair rail and trim along the fireplace mantle. Tan paint lightened the upper sections on two of the walls, while a vintage orange covered the two opposite walls behind the counter and along the fireplace. Between the old wood beams, a light tan coated the ceiling, complimenting the rest of the color scheme.

"The place looks great. I love what a fresh coat of paint can do. I can't believe how dingy and yellow everything had become over the years." Mrs. Collins stepped farther into the room.

"I agree." Uncle Ray grunted. "Keep an open mind, son."

"No." Jack blinked. "Nothing's the same. I can't believe what you've done." He spun again and wanted to push the camera man filming his movements. The invasion of privacy grated his nerves. When he'd agreed to do the makeover, he hadn't understood what he was getting into. Watching *Ryan to the Rescue* had not prepared him for the reality of shooting the episode.

"We experienced issues with the electrical and had to bring the wiring up to code. The new lighting adds to the vintage feel," Sydney answered quietly.

Was she convincing him or herself? He eyed the old-fashioned round lights suspended over the counter and from the wood beams overhead. More antique lights graced the walls, casting a delicate glow in the small space. "I assume I can make changes when you're gone?"

She pursed her lips. "You can do what you want once the filming is done."

An edge filled her voice, but she masked her emotions with a smile. He turned away, his attention shifting to the finer details. Sydney turned the tables on a diagonal, creating an interesting intimate atmosphere and complimenting the splash of colors on the walls. The new wooden chairs were smaller than the original vinyl ones and added a classic coziness to the space.

He walked to the nearest table and glimpsed the old train schedules under the glass. Okay. One thing he agreed to, and he liked the darker stain, which hid the imperfections and made the vintage paper stand out. When he saw the innocent tan fabric underneath the silverware, he jettisoned a hand through his hair again and growled. "Linen napkins!"

"And candles and flowers. How nice. My friends will love this place," Mrs. Collins gushed. Dragging Uncle Ray, Mrs. Collins darted from table to counter.

Jack continued to gape at the new interior. A large vase filled with a juniper branches and red holly berries sat by the cash register, and each table had a small clear vase with the same arrangement in the center. Votive candles lined the fireplace mantle interspersed between Christmas garland, another vase, ribbons, and lights.

Someone had scrubbed the soot, grime, and dirt from the fireplace, exposing the color of the local stones. Then he stared at the fire. No crackle of burning wood. No smoky scent filled his nostrils. He clenched and unclenched his hands. Sydney converted the fireplace to gas. No words formed. Gas burned cleaner, but nothing compared to a real fire. Bile hit the back of his throat.

"Come this way." Sydney motioned. "I used all the photographs of the depot and the town I could find. The railroad crossing signs and train lights came from an antique store in Denver. I've saved the best for last."

She placed a hand on his arm and escorted him to the wall by the front door where painted in cursive on a small panel on one of the old steamer trunks she'd found upstairs was *Thank you for coming. The Ransom Family.*

Tears filled his eyes. Underneath the sign, three pictures framed in ornate antique gold captured his attention. First were his grandparents standing on the porch by the front door. Second was his parents laughing behind the counter. The last one was Jack smiling at Marin, holding a squirmy two-year-old Molly standing by the fireplace. "Where did you find these photos?" His voice came out a gravelly whisper.

"Uncle Ray."

"Thank you." He bowed his head, overwhelmed with emotion. As much as he wanted to stay angry with Sydney, the thought she put into his place stunned him.

"And cut. Good job, people." Philip clapped.

Jack blinked. He'd forgotten about everyone. He

squeezed the bridge of his nose. The cameraman had caught everything on tape again. He couldn't wait until filming was over.

****

Thirty minutes later, Sydney shrugged on her chef jacket and pulled her braids from underneath the fabric to ready herself for her favorite part of filming. While she enjoyed the unveiling of the dining area her designer created, she found her inspiration in food and loved the owners' and staff's reactions when they tasted her dishes. "This next segment was about the food."

"This food should be good," Frank whispered.

"Here's a sneak peek at the new menu." With the laminated menus in the recycle bin, Sydney handed everyone a cream-colored linen paper attached to a piece of thin wood held on by two leather straps.

Jack's jaw tensed, and his lips formed a straight line.

She wouldn't back down. They complemented the restaurant's new concept, along with the updated dishes. "My assistant, Taylor, has prepared samples to familiarize you with the new items."

Jack's eyebrows rose, and his jaw slackened. "You didn't cook the food yourself?"

Sydney shook her head. "Not today. We're running short on time. Right this way."

A woman with a ready smile and black hair tied in a ponytail appeared and set two more plates next to the three already on the counter by the pile of napkins, knives, and forks.

"Thanks, Taylor."

"You're welcome, Sydney." The woman smiled before disappearing into the kitchen.

"In this sequence, Sydney will explain each item and then you try them. The cameras will roll until I call cut. Say what you want. Honesty is always the best." Philip tapped on his phone. "Everyone ready?"

"Yes," the assembled group replied together.

Jack didn't look ready, and Sydney felt sorry, glad the shooting ended tomorrow if everything continued as planned. Then Jack would have two reasons to be happy; filming would be complete, and Sydney and her crew would be on their way to L.A. Again, the end of a production didn't excite her as she waited for the pre-shooting drill to finish.

"And action," the director called.

Sydney didn't miss a stride. "Along with the improved concepts the café offers each morning, I've added five signature dishes that will be a hit with your clientele." She hoped Jack would appreciate the new items as much as he did the photos by the front door. Ignoring the camera, she pointed toward the first plate. "First, we have a natural beef hash with poached eggs and sour dough toast. Next is the breakfast burrito with chorizo and homemade chips and salsa." Sydney motioned to each plate as she described the contents. "Here's the apple pancake with a cinnamon glaze, and over here is the spinach and feta omelet with seven grain toast and fresh fruit. Finally, my favorite, the portabella eggs Benedict with country-style potatoes and fresh fruit. Dig in."

Jack's employees didn't need another invite.

"Try this hash. I've tasted nothing like it." Mrs. Collins crammed another bite into her mouth.

Uncle Ray speared a second piece on his fork. "Same with this apple pancake. I don't know how I'll prepare all these new items."

Max grunted his approval and cut off more of the burrito.

Sydney never doubted the employees' reactions to the new menu items. What Jack thought worried her. Would he agree with his staff, or would he react the same way as he did when he viewed his updated interior?

****

With everyone talking at once, Jack flipped his attention between them, his controlled world tilting off axis.

"Eat, Jack." Mrs. Collins put the fork to his lips.

His server forced him to take a bite. He chewed on the gooey apple concoction and winced in pleasure. Mrs. Collins was right. The pancake was unlike anything he'd ever eaten. He didn't need to try the hash or the burrito to know the items would taste just as good. If Sydney made tofu appetizing, everything she prepared, even granola, would be exceptional.

"Well, what do you think?"

Sydney's smile dazzled him, and he fought the urge to reach for its warmth. Crazy. The woman had turned his life upside down. From the décor to the menu, his restaurant was unrecognizable. "I'll let the customers decide." He ground out.

"Not a problem."

The sparkle disappeared from her eyes before Sydney shifted her gaze. He noticed her swallow, then she recovered and forced a smile for the camera. "And, Jack, here's your new point-of-sale system. No more hard-to-decipher, handwritten orders, no more running to the kitchen to put it in, and no more lost orders." She pointed toward the new machine on the ledge behind the counter.

"Looks complicated. I don't understand this new technology. I'm such a dinosaur." Mrs. Collins huffed.

"You're not, Mrs. Collins. We use a similar one at the hotel. I'll help you." Ally, a server on loan from Larry and Cynthia stepped in beside the older woman.

"Sounds like more work." Frank bunched his towel. "Who'll be responsible to pull off the orders from the thingy-magingy and put them on the wheel?"

Jack rubbed his eyes, eager for this production to finish so Sydney and her crew would leave. Then everything could get back to as normal as it could be with the changes Sydney Ryan had made in both his restaurant, his and Molly's lives.

****

"It's eleven o'clock. Time for the grand opening." Sydney squeezed Jack's arm. "Are you ready?"

As the front house staff stood by the counter, tension bit into his shoulder muscles. "Does that really matter?"

"You're doing great. This is your last segment."

Outside the front door, he saw the line of waiting customers and glimpsed a woman from the production staff collecting the required, signed release forms to appear in the episode.

"I can't believe I'll be on TV." Ally giggled as she smoothed her hair.

Mrs. Collins fanned herself. "I'm glad Larry and Cynthia let us borrow you. With the mob waiting to get inside, I doubt I'd manage."

"I hope everything goes okay with the new menu," said Brianne.

From the looks of things, Jack thanked his lucky stars for his temporary employees.

"I'll be so embarrassed if I drop something." Max used his apron as a towel.

"Everything will be fine. I'll be here to help if needed." Sydney lifted an arm and allowed the sound man to adjust her microphone while the makeup artist dotted more concealer and powder under her eyes.

"Settle down, please." Philip stepped through the front door and moved beside Sydney. "It will get crowded with the customers and crew. There's an overhead mic, and each table has a hidden camera and microphone in the Christmas centerpiece to catch the customer's conversations and expressions. Martin will film out here, and Ricardo will be in the kitchen. Just act natural." Philip clapped. "Places, everyone."

Jack watched Sydney join Philip in the two director's chairs at the far end of the room, away from the action. Unless a catastrophe happened, the rest was up to him and his staff. As he took his position by the front door, Jack shifted. The next three hours would make or break his restaurant. He hoped his staff could handle the task, or he'd look like a fool and could never show his face in town again.

His unease grew at the growing crowd. How would he accommodate everyone? How many people had Sydney invited to this fiasco? He craned his neck to catch a glimpse. She smiled and gave him a thumbs-up. She passed the proverbial spatula, and for Molly's sake, he would not fail.

Time blurred and the next thing he knew, a blast of chilly air hit him when he opened the front door. He blinked and shook his head to focus. Whatever happened, it would soon be over. "Welcome to the new and improved Joe's Café, Mr. and Mrs. Carlson."

Thirty minutes into the service, a commotion erupted from the kitchen, and Ally scrambled through the double doors, her hands in the air.

Mrs. Collins frowned and fiddled with her eyeglass chain as she stared at the POS system.

He heard the crash of breaking glass, and the murmur of conversations grew louder as the customers waited for their food. The crowd outside the door increased. His stomach churned as he strode to the kitchen. He felt Sydney's presence as she entered the kitchen behind him. Jack scratched his neck.

Instead of cooking, Frank and Uncle Ray stood behind the line yelling at each other.

Sydney's panicked assistant worked between the men plating an order.

The clicking sound of another ticket on the new machine added to the chaos that the camera man caught on film.

His kitchen had come to a standstill. Orders piled up as more came in. Frank and Uncle Ray couldn't manage even with the assistant's help. Jack should have spaced the customers, but he didn't want to keep them waiting in the cold. Sydney shouldn't have created a complicated menu. Frank and Uncle Ray were short-order cooks, not trained chefs, and Max almost dropped a stack of dishes he'd pulled from the dishwasher. "What's the problem?" Jack growled.

"I'm not used to this stress. I'm beat." Uncle Ray shook his head. He removed his towel, untied his apron, and threw both items over the side of the trash can. "Sorry, Jack. Can't work anymore. I quit. I should have years ago."

The camera still rolled.

"Uncle Ray, wait."

"Let him go, Jack." Sydney stopped him. "I'm sorry. He was part of your problem."

Pain stabbed his heart. How? Sure, like Mrs. Collins he'd slowed, but he always got out the orders. "Uncle Ray has been a part of this place for years. I couldn't have done it without him."

"He knew that. Why do you think he stayed so long?" Sydney stepped behind the line and tucked the order slip under the tab. "Okay. Taylor, you assist Frank. I'll help Jack. Let's get moving." She cracked two eggs onto the hot griddle. "You might not have seen the signs of fatigue with your uncle, but I've encountered the situation several times."

Jack pulled the toast from the toaster. "Why didn't he say anything?"

Sydney flipped the eggs. "My guess is he didn't want to hurt your feelings. How's the rest of the order?"

"The hash is done, and everything needs to be plated."

Before long, Sydney and Taylor helped Frank and Jack break the gridlock in the kitchen. "Jack? Table six, please?"

He picked up the plates off the line and admired Sydney's presentation. She cut each burrito on a diagonal with one half resting on the other showing the eggs, chorizo, black beans, corn, and tomatoes inside. A scoop of black bean and corn medley, fresh guacamole, and homemade tortilla chips completed the meal with a ramekin of salsa. Instead of fruit, she'd placed a sprig of cilantro and two black olives. His stomach growled.

With the kitchen organized, Jack needed to make sure the front of the house ran as smooth.

After he dropped off the plates for the Joneses, Jack glanced around with renewed interest. Sydney transformed the café from out-of-date and dull, to quaint and cozy, filled with customers eating five-star food who lingered over cups of coffee.

"Jack Ransom, come here, boy." The stylish woman in her mid-sixties waved him over, wearing an enormous grin. She shared the table with a few other women. "The ladies and I love the atmosphere, and the new menu is outstanding. Sydney Ryan has done an amazing job."

The only words that registered in his brain sprung from his lips. "Thanks, Mrs. Peterson." Jack remained in the dining area to gage his customers' reactions. Like his grandparents and parents before him, he believed in greeting his customers by name and being hands-on and available. Jack grabbed the coffee pot and walked onto the floor. "Good morning, Mr. and Mrs. Hart. How is everything today?" He filled their half-empty coffee cups.

"Wonderful. We like the new menu. Fred and I were admiring the interior, and I like the centerpieces. Nice touch." Mrs. Hart dabbed her napkin at the corners of her mouth.

"Thanks." Jack admitted the Mason jar filled with layers of rock salt and cranberries topped with fresh-cut juniper branches in the center of the table looked nice and hid the mini camera and microphone. The linen napkins he hated added an upscale air as did the updated color scheme. He struggled to believe he was in the same space he'd known since he could walk.

Mr. Hart patted his round belly. "Sydney Ryan has done a fabulous job. The omelet and french toast are delicious. We'll have to wait for a table now, or not get a seat at all."

"Don't worry, folks. We'll always have a table for our regulars. Thanks for coming in." Each table he stopped by only had more compliments and more promises to dine in more often and tell all their friends about the new Joe's Café. As he put the pot back on the warmer, Jack's shoulders slumped. Sydney Ryan worked her magic as she'd promised and made his place a successful go-to destination.

All the success in the world meant nothing if he didn't have someone to share it with.

Chapter Fourteen

"It's Santa. It's Santa," Molly squealed and tugged Jack's hand.

She pulled him toward the line of families waiting outside the tiny, one-room building that housed the jolly man in the red suit. Clouds blocked out the moonlight, and snow flurries added to the winter scene in the park surrounding the courthouse. Christmas lights strung around the base of the trees and wrapped around the light poles decorated with wreaths and ribbons added to the festive mood, as did the canned music coming from the stage to his left.

"Do you think Mrs. Claus is here this year? Do you think Ms. Sydney will meet us here like she promised, Daddy? Do you think she'll like our festival?"

"Whoa. One question at a time." His daughter dragged him into line behind a family with a toddler. He pulled his jacket collar around his neck, blocking out the cold; then he did the same for Molly. He should buy her a new scarf, mittens, and a hat to match her new jacket, but finding time to drive to Grand Junction seemed impossible since Sydney's arrival.

Molly clapped her mismatched-mitten-clad hands. "Okay. Do you think Mrs. Claus is here this year?"

Jack leaned to his right to see inside the cozy room where the person hired to play Santa held a young boy on his lap. He didn't recognize the man from town, but the festival organizers hired him every year for the last decade. His white beard was real, and the sparkling blue eyes spoke of someone who loved children and Christmas. His gentle way from the small tots to the giggling teenage girls made him real, even though Jack suspected this year would be the last one where Molly still believed. As the line inched closer, he heard the excitement from the three families behind him.

Moments later, a gray-haired woman holding a basket of candy canes joined Santa.

"Looks like she is."

"Yippee." Molly hooted. "I hope Ms. Sydney makes it in time to see Santa. She is coming, isn't she, Daddy? She didn't change her mind, did she?"

"I'm sure she is because she said so this afternoon. She would have told us if she wasn't. I wonder if she got stuck at the restaurant?" He surveyed the crowded park a few blocks from the center of town. In the mass of people, he'd sense her presence. His Sydney radar hadn't gone off yet, so she was nowhere in the vicinity. As he shuffled ahead a few more feet, the anticipation grew in the surrounding air.

Jack swallowed. He hadn't anticipated something in a long time, and for only one reason. He glanced around the area for Sydney again but only recognized several of his customers and families from Molly's school. A sense of loss pervaded the area. In the short time they'd known each other, Jack had grown accustomed to her smile, her zest for life, and her love for his daughter and his restaurant. Grown accustomed? *Right*. Who was he kidding?

He was falling in love, and it had nothing to do with the magic of the season.

"I hope Ms. Sydney comes. She can't miss the biggest celebration in Silver Ridge. Can I drink hot chocolate while we sing the Christmas carols?"

Grateful for the distraction, Jack returned his attention to his daughter. Her eyes and hair coloring so like Marin's made him pause. Ever since her mother's death, Jack and Molly depended on each other to get through the day. Was he ready for more? Had Uncle Ray, Mrs. Collins, and everyone else in Silver Ridge who told him it was time to move on been right? Had the time come? He would think about dating again, but not now. This evening was for Molly. "Sure. We'll all drink a cup. It will keep our voices warm." As Jack scratched the back of his neck, a funny feeling erupted in his stomach. After he turned and saw Sydney winding her way through the crowd, he released his breath. She might not care about him, which saddened him, but she cared about Molly and wouldn't disappoint her. "See who's here."

"Ms. Sydney, you made it. So did Mrs. Claus. She must have all her chores done at the North Pole." Molly wrapped her arms around Sydney's waist.

Jack wanted to do the same. His mood lightened, and he felt like a schoolboy again with his tongue tied, and his words a jumble inside his brain.

"I promised you I would." Sydney hugged Molly and gave a tentative smile. "Hi, Jack."

She'd worn a sad expression once the day's filming finished. She released Molly and stepped back.

"Glad you're here. Molly's been asking about you." He'd wondered, too, but didn't voice his thought. He didn't like to see her unhappy and wanted to bring back her smile.

"And miss the biggest event of the year?" She shook her head. "No way."

He couldn't pull away his gaze. Redness from the cold infused her cheeks, and her eyes shone in the lights. A pale pink gloss tinted her lips, and wisps of blonde hair escaped from beneath her dark green knitted hat. Her light floral perfume drowned out the wood-burning scent from the nearby fire pits. His heart beat out of rhythm. Sydney made him want to bask in her presence.

She affected other men, too. After a few more appreciative glances from other male residents, he wove an arm through hers and gathered her close. She stiffened but didn't pull away. In fact, he swore she leaned a little closer. They shuffled forward again, and only one family remained ahead. Maybe his daughter wouldn't be the only one to make a request from Santa this year.

A few minutes later, the jolly man patted his knee and motioned for the next child to sit. "Ho, ho, ho. Welcome, Molly. Come in. Don't be shy."

Wide-eyed, Molly surged forward and sat. "You always know my name."

"I do. I know everything about Christmas." Santa's eyes twinkled as he winked at Jack. Returning the wink, he and Sydney settled in the corner of the cozy room.

Sydney squeezed his arm. "How does he know her name?"

"Every year high school girls dress as elves and go through the line quietly asking the name of the children waiting to visit Santa. After a few families, the elves go inside to make sure Santa has everything he needs and then hand him a piece of paper with the information.

This year, the girls are giving it to Mrs. Claus, who will then tell Santa the names and anything special the parents want him to tell their kids. It surprises the kids every year and adds an air of authenticity. Especially the kids who haven't been nice all year long.

"I gave Molly's name before you arrived. Look." Jack pointed to a teenage girl strolling along the line handing out candy canes and smiles. "Marin was an elf the last two years of high school. She'd always looked cute in her costume. I hope Molly will be one, too, when she gets older," Jack whispered and glanced up, imagining a smiling Marin. For the first time, he didn't feel pain.

When he grabbed Sydney's hand, he noticed the perfect fit, as if it had always belonged there. He had trouble remembering why he hadn't tried before.

"That's brilliant." Sydney smiled.

"And the reason Molly comes here. This Santa is the real deal. Listen."

"So, tell Santa, have you been a good girl?" Santa furrowed his brow, but a smile hovered underneath his bushy beard.

Molly nodded and swung her legs back and forth.

"Are you getting good grades?" Santa questioned. "I'm tight with Mrs. Baxter. She and Mrs. Claus are dear friends."

"She's that old?" Molly nodded again, her eyes widening.

Both Santa and Mrs. Claus laughed.

Jack heard Sydney stifle a giggle. The sound was music to his ears. Chuckling, he squeezed her hand. "I told you he was the real deal."

"Are you listening to your parents?" Santa winked

and pushed his wire-rimmed glasses on his nose.

Molly nodded before she whispered into Santa's ear, her hand hiding her lips, and her attention darting between Jack and Sydney.

Obviously, Jack wouldn't need to make a request of Santa.

As he listened to Molly, Santa's expression grew serious. He nodded a few times. "Thanks for sharing. I'll see what the magic Christmas snow can do to make your wish come true." Santa scooped a handful of white glitter in the large basin next to him, whispered a few words, and blew. Glitter floated around Molly. Then he touched a finger to the side of his nose, smiled, and winked. "Ho, ho, ho. Merry Christmas. Dad, would you like to take a picture?"

"Yes." He tapped the camera icon on his cell phone. Molly smiled, and Santa's grin matched the twinkle in his eyes. Jack snapped a few pictures, glad Santa reminded him. Sydney made him forget things.

"Now with you and Ms. Sydney." Molly motioned them to come over.

"Molly, I'll take the picture of you and your dad. This is your time." Sydney protested.

"I want you, too, Ms. Sydney, so I'll always remember you were here. Please?"

"Go on. I'll take it." Mrs. Claus set her basket on the small table, took Jack's phone, and shooed them toward Santa.

Jack agreed. Sydney's time here ended soon, and he also wanted a memory of the reality TV star. He stood on Santa's left and Sydney to his right. Envy almost overtook him when she placed a hand on Santa's shoulder. Jack had it bad. Was he jealous of Santa?

"Okay, now smile. Say candy cane." Mrs. Claus wrinkled her nose and wiggled her ample hips, so the bells sewn on her red dress jingled.

"Candy cane," the four of them said together while Mrs. Claus captured the memory.

"Now Mrs. Claus has something special for you out back, Molly, so run along. Your dad and Ms. Sydney will join you in a minute."

After his daughter left with Santa's pretend wife, Jack saw him motion them to stay.

He put one hand on his belly, while his other hand played with his beard. He shuttled his gaze between them, his eyes twinkling as a frown pursed his lips.

Jack shifted his weight, waiting to be chastised by the man in the red suit. The last time that happened he was twelve years old and about to get in trouble for toilet papering old man Benito's house. Sydney's presence steadied him.

Santa continued to stroke his beard. "Your daughter is very perceptive and precocious, and I love her. She's been sad the past few years, and now I understand. I'm sorry for her loss, and yours, too, Dad. I'm sure you know what she's asking for. There are things I can't do. I'm Santa, not Cupid, but I'll try." Santa scooped more glitter, stood, whispered a few words, and blew the fake snow all over them. "Good luck and Merry Christmas."

"Merry Christmas to you, too, Santa. Thank you."

What Jack suspected about Molly's wish was true. Santa was right. He could only do so much in matters of the heart. Despite his earlier thoughts, Jack wasn't quite ready to take another chance.

****

Jack's hand on Sydney's arm created mixed emotions as she stepped outside Santa's house so the next family could have their turn. Mixed emotions battled for space in every fiber of her being. She'd known upon meeting Molly the little girl wanted a stepmom. Sydney loved Molly, and as she viewed Jack's profile, she realized she loved him.

Nothing would become of this one-sided romance, despite what Emily hoped. Sydney lived in L.A. Jack and Molly lived here. No wedding bells or bouquets were in her future. She had a contract to renew and her own restaurant to open in a few years.

Her thoughts cast a shadow over the night's festivities, and her holiday spirit snapped in the chilly, still night. Despite Santa's best efforts, no Christmas magic would happen, and like every other year for the past decade, she'd escape to another lonely beach.

Moments later, Molly met them, wearing an impish grin and carrying a few more candy canes. "What did you ask Santa for, Daddy?"

Smiling, Jack tweaked his daughter's nose. "None of your business. Like birthday wishes, Santa requests are confidential. Now what do you want to do?"

Molly grabbed their hands. "Drink hot chocolate and sing Christmas carols. Let's go."

"I can't wait to hear Ms. Sydney sing. She told me she sings like Maria von Trapp." Jack squeezed her arm.

The twinkle in his voice and his wink confused her. Something had changed. Had the glitter been magic Christmas snow? Nonsense. His crooked smile only added more sadness.

"Is that true?" Molly tugged at her hand.

Sydney shook off her melancholy mood. Molly deserved for her to be in better spirits tonight. Filming had wrapped, and tomorrow afternoon, she'd be on her way back to L.A. "My talents are fixing restaurants and cooking, not singing. What I said to your father was I wanted to sound like Maria, not like a frog."

"Then you and my dad are alike. Uncle Ray says my daddy could shatter the windows in the café if he sang loud enough, and he wasn't kidding," Molly announced.

When she peeked at Jack for guidance, she caught his grin that made her insides melt.

He shrugged. "You can't attend the festival unless you take part. That's the rules. If I have to sing, you do, too."

"Come on. Let's go." Molly dragged them toward the booth selling drinks.

Her enthusiasm was almost contagious. Sydney had no interest in singing and would rather listen to the Christmas carols with the light snow flurries in the man's company who made her heart beat faster.

"They're starting any minute. There's Sam. Over here," Molly called and waved.

Hot chocolates in hand, Jack sat on an empty hay bale in front of one of the fire pits stationed around the park's common area. The fire's heat warmed her, but it couldn't compare to Jack's sizzling look. The soft orange glow danced across his angular features, heightening her awareness. She had a difficult time remembering why she needed to keep her emotions intact, although she suspected that ship had sailed when she met him.

Jack entwined their fingers and squeezed. "Thanks

for coming tonight."

With Molly visiting with Sam and her family, Sydney squeezed back, her breath hitching in her throat, as she stared into his eyes. She fought the urge to pull off her glove and touch the roughness of his five o'clock shadow. She swallowed. "I wouldn't miss it for the world. Thanks for inviting me."

"It was Molly's idea, but I'm glad she thought of it." He raised her gloved hand and brushed his lips across her knuckles. "Believe it or not, despite our differences, I enjoy our time together."

"I do, too." Sydney broke the fragile thread. The deep emotions welling inside left her confused and disoriented. "Except I don't look forward to singing."

"Me either, but God gave me this voice, so he may as well hear it. We'll have fun. I promise." He squeezed her hand again.

"If you say so." Sydney watched the flames consume the logs inside the metal pit. The fire's crackle and pop drowned the surrounding sounds while the smoke mingled with Jack's earthy cologne. Soft snowflakes drifted across her vision, reminding her of her first conversation with Molly.

She glanced at the cloudy sky. The angels worked overtime tonight to create the Christmas atmosphere. That thought gave her courage, and she was almost out of time. She gazed at Jack and swallowed. "I need to tell you something."

As he pursed his lips, a shadow crossed over his features. "You're going back to L.A."

"We're done. Our flight leaves late tomorrow afternoon. Taylor will stay a few extra days to help you learn the new recipes." Sydney took a deep breath.

"Also, your Uncle Ray didn't quit. That scene was scripted to add conflict. He'll be there in the morning. Phillip also told him to have two left thumbs to slow down things."

He raised his eyebrows. "So, reality TV isn't real."

A melancholy smile creased her lips. "Most of it is. We never know what people will say or how everything will put together."

"Do you have to leave?" Jack leaned in. "Can't you stay through the holidays? It would mean a lot to Molly." Jack leaned in.

His breath warm against her skin, Sydney dug a heel into the ground, disappointed. "I have to respond to fan letters and negotiate a new contract. I also have to put out a few fires that cropped up while I was here."

"So, this is good-bye." He pulled off his glove and stroked her face. He lifted her chin and kissed her lips. "Thanks for saving our restaurant, Sydney. I don't know how to repay you."

Sydney blinked, never imagining she'd ever hear those words pass his lips. But they weren't the words she wanted him to say. "No thanks necessary, but you're welcome. Fixing restaurants is what I do best." Moisture filling her eyes, she turned her cheek into his palm. "I'm leaving a few Christmas presents at the hotel for you and Molly. Open them any time."

His voice softened to a whisper as he caressed her face. "You didn't need to buy us anything."

Warmth filled her. "Yes, I did. Do me a favor and don't tell Molly until we're gone? I hate long good-byes."

"So do I."

Sydney didn't want to leave, but she had to. Her

life was in L.A., and theirs was in Silver Ridge. Aside from Molly, Jack also hadn't given her a reason to stay, so in a few weeks, she'd be on the beach with a new five-year contract for *Ryan to the Rescue*. More sadness consumed her.

****

Mid-morning on Sunday, Sydney shook the snow globe and watched the white flakes swirl around the angel inside. Tears welled. She knew she'd found the perfect gift for Molly. Resting her forehead on the cool glass, she asked the angel to watch over and take care of Jack's daughter. After she planted a light kiss on the surface and placed the globe back inside the box, she pulled out a small Christmas card purchased from the same shop.

Merry Christmas, Molly.
Now your mom can make snow for you throughout the year.
Love, Ms. Sydney

After tucking the card next to the globe, she arranged Molly's matching hat, scarf, and mittens in a shirt box. Jack's gift of his own matching set of a scarf and gloves received the same careful attention. As she wrapped the boxes in festive Santa paper, she wiped her tears.

She'd never dreaded leaving a location before. Was it Silver Ridge or two of the quaint town's occupants? After she finished, she wandered to the window and glanced at Joe's Café, knowing the restaurant was out of her hands. She had an excellent success track record, but a few had failed, and she hoped Jack's place wouldn't be one of them. After letting the lace curtain

215

fall, she strode back to the bed, packed her suitcase, and checked her room one last time.

In the lobby, Sydney walked to the front desk and rang the bell.

Moments later, Cynthia appeared from the office. "Sydney. Is it time for you to leave?"

"Yes, believe it or not." She placed her key on the counter and forced a smile.

The owner returned one of her own. "Larry and I talked about you last night. We hoped you'd stay through the holidays. You've been such a breath of fresh air." She pulled a piece of paper from the printer and set it on the counter. "Sign here, please."

Taking the proffered pen, Sydney signed her name and slid it back. "I'd love to, but I have to get back. I've got to take care of business."

Cynthia placed a duplicate on the counter. "Here's your copy. We're sorry to see you go, and we won't forget what you've done for the town. I'm sure I speak for the entire population when I say we can't wait to see the episode."

"Thanks, Cynthia. You and Larry were wonderful hosts." Sydney produced her business card. "If you need more advice, call or email. I'll always be happy to help."

Six hours later, Sydney drank from the bottle of water she bought at the Denver airport. Even with most of her crew on the same flight, she never felt more alone. She couldn't help thinking she was making a huge mistake as the miles increased the distance between the life she never knew she wanted, and the life she'd grown accustomed to.

A tear slid down her cheek. She missed Jack and

Molly, and the thought of never seeing them again tore her emotions to shreds. But Jack didn't love her, and Sydney couldn't compete with the memories of Marin.

Chapter Fifteen

"Sydney Ryan, my office, now." Becca leaned in Sydney's office and motioned for her to follow.

With a sense of déjà vu, she glanced from the stack of fan letters. Had only a few weeks passed since her producer ordered her to go to Silver Ridge and find Molly at Joe's Café?

So much had happened. She'd pulled off the makeover, the filming, and contract negotiations were underway. The biggest surprise was Sydney fell in love. Despite her friends and crew, loneliness crept in at the worst time. Like now. An office full of people, but the two people she wanted to see lived over a thousand miles away. Sadness consumed her, knowing she'd get a glimpse of Jack during the sneak preview of the episode before it aired next week.

"Coming." Sydney stood. The letters could wait another hour, but she would answer all of them before she left on vacation, even though the pile seemed to have quadrupled overnight. Her devotion to her fans would be another point to bring into the negotiations.

"Have a seat." Becca quit tapping her keyboard. "How are you doing? You look tired."

"I'm fine." Sydney set the binders from the chair on the floor. Becca's office remained disorganized. "How about you? You're showing."

Before she pulled another soda cracker from the

wrapper, Becca massaged her stomach. "I'm glad I didn't donate my maternity clothes. I'll be a whale by summer. When I go to the beach, people will try and roll me back into the ocean."

"I think they'd know the difference." Sydney laughed for the first time in over a week. She stared outside. With a week until Christmas, the sun shone, the palm trees swayed in the breeze, and the temps hovered in the high sixties. So unlike Silver Ridge with the mountains, pine trees, and snow.

Becca repositioned her computer to face the screen outward, making it easier to view. "I wanted your thoughts on the actress hired to read Mary-Katerina's letter. Ready?"

"As ready as I'll ever be." Sydney fisted her hands. Apprehension gripped her, unsure about the final edit because she loved Jack and Molly.

"Here we go." Becca pushed Play and wedged her hip on the side of her desk.

Christmas music filled the air, and the title displayed overtop the backdrop of Silver Ridge filling the screen. Christmas lights twinkled in the garland-wrapped light poles and the trees lining the main street. The red bows welcomed the tiny flakes of snow, and darkness crowded out the fading sunlight draping the sky in purple and blue. More lights glowed in the shop windows surrounded by more twinkling lights and wreaths. The camera panned to take in the Grand Hotel dressed in its Christmas glory. In front, Tom tipped his hat from his seat in the same carriage that drove them for a ride the night of their dinner.

An avalanche of emotion hit Sydney. She'd never felt so at home in a place, which made her longing to return to Silver Ridge more painful. She hoped Jack, Frank, and Uncle Ray were doing okay with her recipes. Her assistant, Taylor, worked with them for a week but returned concerned the cooks might not be consistent in their reproduction.

Sydney tried her best, but were her efforts enough, so Jack had a legacy to leave to Molly? After the opening sequence, the actress appeared sitting on the hearth of a stone fireplace. Dark, curly hair framed her face and her wide, blue eyes reminded her of Molly. She blinked. "Wow. Casting did an excellent job based on my description."

"That was easy. The challenge was finding the stone fireplace." Becca sighed and reached for another cracker. "I know the ratings will be high, and it might be your best episode to date."

"I'll hold you to those words during the final contract negotiations."

"Good luck. Can't hold a pregnant woman responsible for what she says when she's in the middle of morning sickness." Her producer chewed her cracker. "I see something different about you in this episode. I can't put my finger on it." The rest of the cracker disappeared. She scratched her head. "You seemed…almost radiant during the filming. I've seen nothing like it."

She waited for Becca to comment on the kitchen scene with Jack. Emily confirmed both her producers had seen him stroke her cheek. Was that why Becca wasn't herself this morning? This pregnancy was different, so this one had to be a boy. "What you saw was my reaction to the cold weather, nothing more."

"Right. Okay, keep watching."

The sincerity in her voice as she read the letter brought tears to Sydney's eyes. Becca and Marv made the right decision. This idea was the magical touch for a Christmas special; the girl, the town, the decorations, but the child wasn't Molly, and Sydney felt like an intruder, an interloper into Jack and his daughter's lives.

Jack looked amazing with his dark, unruly hair in much need of a trim. She drank in the sight of him. His blue eyes mesmerized her as did the five o'clock shadow hugging his cheeks. Almost too perfect, but nowhere near the emotional and intellectual level that existed underneath his gruff exterior. And for a reason. She'd forced herself and her ideas upon them. Her vision, not Jack's, which became clear the longer she watched the show. White knuckles gleamed in the office light as she gripped the chair and squirmed. "Who edited this episode?"

"Charlie Whitmore. Why?" Becca folded her arms under her breasts.

"The show is horrible, Becca, and it doesn't do justice to Joe's Café or Jack." Sydney fought the urge to jump from her chair and pace. She remained seated, riveted to the computer screen, listening to the words the editor spliced into sentences. Jack never uttered anything close to those words. Her stomach nosedived to the floor.

Like a moth to flame, she couldn't pull away her gaze, each scene worse than the previous one. If Jack's employees felt the way they expressed, why had they never told him? Why did they expose Jack's private life on television? "When did they film the on-the-fly interviews with Frank and Ray?"

"Not sure, but they hit the nail on the head."

"The restaurant wasn't that bad, Becca. Trust me." Things had needed work; the restaurant had been stuck in the seventies and the food needed help with the items and presentation... Sydney slumped back in her chair. She sounded like Jack.

"True, but you know the employee interviews make the show more interesting. We've done them every episode. The beats, too. What's wrong?" Her producer stared and ate another cracker.

"Maybe I'm developing a heart. Go back to the drawing room floor. Use different footage. Unlike the person portrayed here, Jack's kind and caring. He's not...an ogre."

Becca shook her head. "Too late."

Bile hit the back of her throat. Unable to sit, Sydney stood and paced the office confines. She'd promised Jack the show would highlight him and the town in a positive light. This episode made him look like a jerk and an idiot, and he'd be the laughingstock of Silver Ridge. How many other owners had she humiliated for her own personal gain? "Pull it. Use the original piece you bumped, or I'll walk."

She opened and shut her mouth. "I can't pull the episode. Now, I'm speaking as a friend and not your producer. You're in contract negotiations for another five years, Sydney. Don't be a fool. This isn't the first time an owner has looked bad or been thrown under the bus by his or her employees. It won't be the last. That's the nature of this business."

Sydney heard enough. She wouldn't be a part of reality TV any longer, and if she ever saw Jack again, she hoped he'd forgive her. "That's not acceptable anymore. Good-bye, Becca. I quit."

****

In a sleep-deprived haze, Jack wandered through the restaurant kitchen. He rubbed his eyes. He had orders to cook and dishes to run through the dishwasher, but he had no clue where to start. With Frank out, Uncle Ray worked behind the line after ordering him to leave.

"Don't just stand there, I need eggs." Uncle Ray motioned toward the cooler and flipped the french toast. "Then I need you to plate food."

Jack stumbled into the walk-in and stared at the shelves. A chill descended as he scratched the back of his neck. Why did he come in here? Since Sydney returned to L.A., he'd been a walking zombie, going through the motions of living, but dead inside. His daughter wasn't any better. Sydney left ten days ago, and yet her absence felt like ten years.

"What did Uncle Ray need?" He stared at the shelves. "Yogurt? No. More hash? Not that. Bacon? No." He still had a tray left. To his right on a lower shelf, he spied a green-and-white package. Where had that come from? The tofu reminded him of Sydney, even though she never strayed far from his thoughts. He picked up the package. What he wouldn't give for one of her tacos.

His stomach growled, reminding him he'd hardly eaten for the last week and a half. He could also go for her beef hash, which even with the assistant's help he'd been unable to duplicate, despite Sydney's recipe and instructions. Frustration kicked in, and he struck the metal shelving with his foot. The hash wasn't the only thing he couldn't cook. All her specials turned out mediocre. No amount of effort could produce the same results.

Christmas magic? More like Sydney magic. And he was the Scrooge. He should have given her a reason to stay.

The walk-in door opened.

"Did you get lost? I need those eggs. What's in your hand?" Uncle Ray barked.

"Tofu." Jack retrieved a carton of eggs and walked past the old man. He stopped once on his way behind the line to drop the package of tofu in the garbage can because Sydney hadn't left her recipe for the tacos. Once he set the eggs on the counter, he washed his hands. What he wouldn't give to see her beautiful smile and feel her enthusiasm for his restaurant.

"Plate the hash," Frank grumbled as Jack ran into him behind the line. He wasn't the only one that missed her.

Sydney. How was she doing? Did she think about them? Did she fare any better? He missed her. After wiping his forehead with his sleeve, Jack pulled a plate from the shelf above his head. He slopped the food and dropped the orange slice and strawberry by the scrambled eggs.

"Looks terrible, Ransom. Have pride. Fix the garnish." Uncle Ray shoved the plate back in front of him.

"I have pride."

"Then act like it. Sydney Ryan turned this place into a gold mine. Don't ruin it. Don't fail."

Jack watched his uncle twist the orange slice on the plate.

Then he set the stemless strawberry on the flat side.

Uncle Ray dinged the bell, signaling Mrs. Collins to pick up her order. "That's how it's done."

"For goodness' sake, Jack, call her." Mrs. Collins grabbed the plates. "If you had a smart bone in your body, you'd go after her. If you don't do it for your sake, do it for Molly's."

With a clean kitchen rag, Uncle Ray wiped a drop of gravy from the rim of the last plate of the order. "He doesn't have a smart bone in his body. If he did, he would have convinced her to stay."

"He would have packed his bags and followed her." Mrs. Collins huffed.

Exhausted and tired of all his employees' bashing, Jack threw his towel on the counter. "Right. Convince her to stay when her life is there and ours is here. Ask her to give up her career to live in Silver Ridge and settle to work in a small café no one has ever heard about?" He'd run the scenario through his mind many times. "Follow her, Mrs. Collins? How? Rip Molly from the only place she's ever known? Who would run the restaurant?"

Mrs. Collins stared at Uncle Ray. "Molly will be fine, and Ray and I can run the restaurant."

"Or we can buy the place after we're married." The old man placed the ticket under the last plate on the shelf to complete that order.

"What? Married? You two?" Jack widened his eyes as he thrust a hand through his hair. Surprised didn't even come close to the feelings inside.

"Do you have a problem? I know you've been preoccupied, but I thought you would have noticed things months ago. Sydney picked up on it in her first few days." Mrs. Collins pulled the three plates from the shelf, positioned one on her arm, and the other two in her hands.

"Congratulations. When's the big day?" Jack managed to say. He had noticed something between them, he just hadn't realized it was so serious.

"Haven't decided yet. We were waiting until you remarried, but we're running out of time." Uncle Ray used his pointer finger to scroll through the next order. "A number one with scrambled and sausage, and a hash with eggs over easy."

"I'll make the eggs." Jack washed his hands as his uncle placed two sausage patties on the grill. He cracked two eggs as hope and fear warred to take control of his emotions. Sweat gathered under his arms and on his forehead, and his breathing became shallow. His heart ached. He wanted to see Sydney again and on a permanent basis.

"Call Sydney's studio." Mrs. Collins disappeared through the service door.

His uncle and server were right. He needed to fight for what he wanted, and he wanted Sydney in his life and in Molly's, too. Life guaranteed only death and taxes. He'd loved once and lost his wife, which made him afraid to love again. At what cost? He'd let a wonderful woman slip through his fingers because of his fear, stubbornness, pig-headedness, and the other adjectives Sydney spouted.

Love meant taking chances and putting his heart out there again. "Uncle Ray, are you serious about buying the restaurant if Molly and I move to L.A.?"

****

"Everything Home Network, how may I direct your call?" A woman's voice floated over the line.

Jack clenched the office phone and forced away the bile. Nerves wouldn't get the better of him. He cleared his throat and rested his feet on the wooden chair Sydney sat in a few weeks ago. He missed her smiling face, her positive attitude, her love for his restaurant, and the loving care she put into the design and the new menu. "Sydney Ryan, please?"

He twisted the cord around his pointer finger, waiting. A heartbeat passed in silence, and he swore he heard muffled voices. Pulling his feet from the chair, he sat straight and then rested an elbow on the scarred desk. He picked up a pen and doodled her name in blue ink.

"Who may I ask is calling?" a different woman asked.

"Jack Ransom." His heart sank. She didn't want to talk. Beyond the closed door, he heard the clink of silverware on the new plates and the hum of conversation…all because of Sydney Ryan. Even though the episode hadn't aired, word spread through Silver Ridge and Summit Falls that Joe's Café had undergone a renovation.

"I'm sorry, sir, she's not in the office. Is there someone else who can help you?" the second woman responded.

The tone of her voice made him pause. Something wasn't right. He had a sixth sense about those things. He knew each time Molly was getting sick, and he knew about Marin's cancer before she did. What was wrong with Sydney? He squeezed the bridge of his nose and shut his eyes. "When will she be in?"

"I'm not sure. I think she left on vacation."

A noise erupted before complete silence. She must

have put a hand over the receiver. Before she did, he swore she used his name and Sydney's in the same sentence.

"Jack Ransom?" a third woman's voice questioned.

How many people worked in the reception area? Jack figured the network employed a lot of people, but this delay was ridiculous. He ruffled his hair again, figuring he'd run into a few problems connecting with Sydney, but it shouldn't be this hard. "Yes."

"Becca Montgomery. Sydney's former producer."

Ice dripped from her words. Jack bolted to his feet. His chair banged against the desk before wobbling to the floor. "What do you mean former?"

"I don't know what happened out there, but Sydney broke her contract and quit. She's gone."

The phone clicked, and a dial tone filled his ear. Rubbing a hand across his face, he slumped against the desk. A hollow feeling took hold and refused to release its grip. Because of him, Sydney left the job she loved.

****

"Ryan, get in here. Now. We have an issue at the studio you need to fix." Becca barked into the phone.

"No can do, Becca. I quit remember?" Sydney packed an extra tank shirt into her suitcase. In twenty-four hours, she'd be lying on the beach in the Caymans, basking in the sun. With no job now, she didn't need to return.

"If I ever meant anything to you, then you'll come."

"Is it the baby?" Sydney sank on her bed. Despite leaving the network, she hoped she and Becca would remain friends.

"Yes, it concerns a child. I need you here, ASAP."

"Give me half an hour." Sydney sighed and closed her suitcase. She'd finish packing her toiletries tomorrow before the shuttle drove her to LAX.

Twenty minutes later, Claudia, the newest intern, waited at Becca's door. "Hi, Ms. Ryan. She's in A. The light's on, but go in anyway."

Sydney nodded. Her former producer had never been so secretive. Nostalgia coursed through her as she walked the hallway toward the studio. What did Becca have up her sleeve? When she walked through the door, two familiar figures caught her eye. Sydney halted, blinked, and shook her head. Impossible. Her mouth gaped, but no words tumbled out. All noise and action ceased to exist.

"Ms. Sydney, over here." Molly squealed and waved from her chair. A piece of paper fluttered to the floor.

Her heart sank, and butterflies took flight in her stomach. She rubbed her eyes and leaned against the door for support. "Jack? Molly? What are you doing here?"

"You left before we gave you our Christmas present." Molly jumped from her seat and ran to her. She squeezed Sydney's waist, her body shaking with emotion. "I missed you."

"I missed you, too, sweetie." Sydney spoke to Molly as she cradled her, but she froze her gaze on Jack standing next to the chair he'd occupied moments earlier. He clenched and unclenched his hands as if fighting for control.

"I missed you, too, Sydney." Jack found his voice, but he remained planted to the small piece of real estate by the chair.

"What are you doing here?" Sydney knew she looked like a fish out of water as she gasped for air. Her body trembled, and her mind floundered as she tried to comprehend what was happening.

"Your producer, Becca, invited us. You missed a vital piece. We got on the first flight we could. Flying's a little crazy right now."

"I imagine it would be." Sydney glanced around the studio.

Martin and Ricardo waved. Philip nodded and gave a thumbs-up.

Molly pulled away and stared at Sydney with wide eyes. "I've never flown on an airplane. It was so cool. I talked to the captain and copilot and the flight attendants and everything."

"Flying is the best way to travel. I'm glad you liked it." Sydney focused on Jack again. "You never answered my question. Why are you here?" She wanted to ask if he'd seen the episode, and if so, his thoughts. Maybe that's what they were reshooting. Was Becca wrong, and changes could be made? Sydney never guessed she'd see Jack and Molly again, and they'd flown from Denver to make it happen. Hope and love grabbed hold of her heart and pushed away the hurt and loneliness of the past weeks. Tears hovered at the back of her eyes.

"Because you didn't film me reading my letter." Molly grabbed her hand and headed toward her father.

With hesitant steps, Sydney walked toward the man who made her heartbeat race and her breathing a chore. Everyone in the room disappeared so that only the three of them remained. The symptoms elevated the closer she got to Jack. She'd missed him so much.

Every waking hour and in her dreams his face hovered in her consciousness. She could no longer deny her feelings. She loved him since that first day.

"You didn't want Molly on camera," Sydney croaked, standing in front of him. Jack looked good, despite the dark circles under his eyes and the air of despair. Her appearance wasn't any better since she hadn't gotten a decent night's sleep since her return. Even Molly wore a hesitant expression the longer the silence stretched.

"I changed my mind. It wouldn't be the same without Molly reading her letter. We came to film that part." Jack's voice wavered.

She frowned, wanting to reach out and push the wayward piece of hair covering his eyes, not believing that was the real reason they were here. "Have you seen the show?"

"We did. Not bad if I say so myself. I expected worse." A fraction of a smile formed.

"Not bad? You didn't see the same show I did." She protested, unable to calm the queasiness in her stomach.

"He did," Becca interjected. "The segment wasn't that bad."

"Not enough to quit your show," Jack agreed.

Her producer grinned. "So there. Your office is still available when you're ready to return after the holidays. You're expected in New Mexico next month."

"I'm not coming back, Becca." Her life had changed in Silver Ridge and so had Sydney. She wasn't the same person and discovered different goals and needs. Did Jack's being here mean more than bringing Molly to film her reading the letter? He didn't know she loved him and wanted to grow old with him, but he would soon enough, if they ditched their audience. She itched to caress his face and touch his lips, but she forced her hands to remain by her sides.

"May I ask you a question?" With a quick smile, Jack pulled a box from his pocket and knelt. His hands trembled as he held out a small, white jewelry box and opened the lid where an exquisite, oval-shaped sapphire surrounded by tiny diamonds lay inside. "Sydney, I love you. Will you marry me?"

Molly kneeled next beside her dad and tugged her hand again. "Ms. Sydney, I love you, too. Will you become my stepmom?"

Speechless, Sydney ping-ponged her gaze between Jack and Molly. The love shining from both sets of eyes overwhelmed her. She covered her mouth as tears hit the back of her eyelids. Her lips refused to work, and her body shook with emotion as she stared at the kneeling man.

"Please? I love you. I need you. I haven't been able to sleep, or concentrate, or do anything since you left." Jack shifted his weight. "Besides, I'm selling the restaurant to Uncle Ray. Molly and I won't know what to do here if you don't show us."

"If you don't say yes, Uncle Ray and Mrs. Collins will skin him alive, whatever that means," Molly added.

Sydney focused Jack's words, her pulse racing as a lump formed in her throat. "You're doing what?"

"Uncle Ray and the future Mrs. Donaldson offered to buy the place since I can't be an absentee owner from a thousand miles away." Jack pulled the ring from the box. "I know this isn't the most romantic place to propose, but, Sydney Ryan, you brought happiness back to our lives. You made me believe in the forever again when I fell in love with you. Will you marry me?"

"And be my stepmom?" Blinking fast, Molly tugged again.

"Say yes, Sydney, or Uncle Ray and Mrs. Collins won't be the only ones to skin you alive. Since your return, you've been impossible and miserable. You quit because of him. Say yes and give us a real reason to let you out of your contract." Becca folded her arms and raised her eyebrow, a grin twisting her lips.

Sydney shifted her gaze back to Jack and Molly. When she awoke this morning, she'd never imagined her life would spin a three-sixty in a matter of moments. Jack loved her, and she loved him. "I will. I love you, too." Sydney held out her finger and let Jack slip on the ring. "It's beautiful." She wrapped her arms around his neck and kissed him. Tears flowed amidst the applause from the production crew, Becca and Emily vying to be the loudest.

A few moments later, Sydney broke free of Jack's embrace. "But I don't have a job, and you don't own a restaurant anymore, what will we do?"

Jack shrugged and grinned. "We'll figure out something."

Jack leaned forward and took possession of her lips again, his touch soft and tender. Sydney never wanted the moment to end.

The camera caught everything.

Epilogue

"Look, Daddy, Ms. Sydney, it's Santa. It's Santa! Santa. Over here." Molly dragged Jack and Sydney to the man with a white beard and round belly waiting at the same luggage carousel at the Denver airport on Christmas Eve.

Canned Christmas music filled the air as Jack's apology froze on his lips. Staring at the man dressed in the brown, tweed jacket, white shirt, dark slacks, and a black bowler hat, Jack recognized him as the Santa from the festival in Silver Ridge. He glanced around for a family, but the old man traveled alone. *Strange*.

"Hello, Molly. So good to see you again." The man smiled as he winked.

"Sydney. Jack." He tipped his hat.

Jack's lips pursed. How did *Santa* know his name? He only recalled mentioning Molly's. Could it be? *Nah*. He shook his head. *Impossible*. He quit believing years ago. Santa wasn't real, was he? He glanced at Sydney and drew his brows together.

She shrugged, her eyes sparkling under her raised eyebrows. At her warm, generous smile, he forgot everything except for his need to kiss her. He might have if they'd been in private. Having her love made him the luckiest man alive.

With Sydney, he found the courage to love again. She brought back his passion for his restaurant. She made him a better father and as soon as they arranged the ceremony, she would make him a better husband.

He couldn't wait to start their lives together. After hearing the good news, Uncle Ray and Suzette decided to retire in Arizona, and Jack and Sydney would reopen as the R&R Café for Ransom and Ryan.

Molly tugged at Santa's hand. "Santa, why are you here? Why aren't you dressed? Why aren't you at the North Pole getting ready?"

"Ho, ho, ho, Molly, you sure ask a lot of questions." He knelt and tweaked Molly's nose. "My head elf and reindeer are meeting me here because I missed my flight to Alaska this morning. I'm not dressed because I didn't want anyone to recognize me, but I see that didn't work. Children who believe always seem to spot me. Grown-ups do, too." He gave another nod and smile to Jack and Sydney. "As soon as Dash gets here, I'm off to the North Pole to pack my sleigh and deliver presents to the good boys and girls all over the world." Santa stood and looked at his cell phone. He drew his eyebrows together. "The boys are running late. Traffic over the city." He tsked. "This delay will put me behind tonight."

Molly gave him a huge grin. "You don't have to stop at our house, Santa. You've already given me my present. Will that save you time?"

"A few seconds at least. That's very thoughtful." The old man put his finger to his nose, smiled, and winked. "Merry Christmas, Molly." He pulled a small bag of white glitter from his pocket, poured some into his hand, and blew it over the three of them before disappearing into the crowd.

For a moment, Jack wondered if he'd imagined the

whole thing until he saw the glitter shimmering in Molly's and Sydney's hair.

Christmas magic.

Jack slipped an arm around Sydney's shoulders as his chest expanded. He believed.

Molly hugged Jack and Sydney. "All my classmates are wrong. Santa is real. I knew he was, and he brought me a stepmom for Christmas. Thank you, Santa."

A word about the author…

At twelve years old, Kira read her first romance novel and was hooked on the happily ever after endings. For years, she dreamed of writing her own romance stories, and that dream finally came true in 2003.

Based in sunny Arizona, Kira has published numerous books, short stories, and blog articles.

www.kira-anderson.com

Thank you for purchasing
this publication of The Wild Rose Press, Inc.

For questions or more information
contact us at
info@thewildrosepress.com.

The Wild Rose Press, Inc.
www.thewildrosepress.com

www.ingramcontent.com/pod-product-compliance
Lightning Source LLC
Chambersburg PA
CBHW060548260626
47161CB00003B/1112